One of Those HIDEOUS BOOKS Where the Mother Dies

ALSO BY SONYA SONES

What My Mother Doesn't Know

What My Girlfriend Doesn't Know

One of Those HIDEOUS BOOKS Where the Mother Dies

SONYA SONES

SIMON & SCHUSTER BFYR
New York London Toronto Sydney New Delhi

SIMON & SCHUSTER BFYR
An imprint of Simon & Schuster Children's Publishing Division
1230 Avenue of the Americas, New York, New York 10020
This book is a work of fiction. Any references to historical events, real people, or real places are used fictitiously. Other names, characters, places, and events are products of the author's imagination, and any resemblance to actual events or places or persons, living or dead, is entirely coincidental.
Copyright © 2004 by Sonya Sones
All rights reserved, including the right of reproduction
in whole or in part in any form.
SIMON & SCHUSTER BFYR is a trademark of Simon & Schuster, Inc.
For information about special discounts for bulk
purchases, please contact Simon & Schuster Special Sales at
1-866-506-1949 or business@simonandschuster.com.
The Simon & Schuster Speakers Bureau can bring authors to your live event. For more information or to book an event, contact the Simon & Schuster Speakers Bureau at 1-866-248-3049 or visit our website at www.simonspeakers.com.
Also available in a SIMON & SCHUSTER BFYR hardcover edition.
Book design by Ann Zeak
The text for this book is set in Oranda BT.
Manufactured in the United States of America
This SIMON & SCHUSTER BFYR paperback edition May 2013
10 9 8 7 6 5 4 3 2 1
The Library of Congress has cataloged the hardcover edition as follows:
One of those hideous books where the mother dies / by Sonya Sones.—1st ed.
p. cm.
Summary: Fifteen-year-old Ruby Milliken leaves her best friend, her boyfriend, her aunt, and her mother's grave in Boston and reluctantly flies to Los Angeles to live with her father, a famous movie star who divorced her mother before Ruby was born.
ISBN 978-0-689-85820-8 (hc)
[1. Fathers and daughters—Fiction. 2. Moving, household—Fiction. 3. Actors and actresses—Fiction. 4. Grief—Fiction. 5. Interpersonal relations—Fiction. 6. Homosexuality—Fiction. 7. Los Angeles (Calif.)—Fiction.] I. Title.
PZ7.S6978 Mi 2004
[Fic]—dc21   2003009355
ISBN 978-1-4424-9383-4 (pbk)
ISBN 978-1-4391-0757-7 (eBook)

for Bennett
with love and admiration

Heartfelt thanks to Ruth Bornstein, Peg Leavitt, Betsy Rosenthal, Ann Wagner, and April Halprin Wayland, for your generosity and your brilliance. Deepest of curtsies to Myra Cohn Livingston, David Gale, Russell Gordon, and Steven Malk, for making it all possible. Tons of gratitude to my kind readers, for the glowing e-mails that have kept me afloat. And huge hugs and kisses to Ava and Jeremy, for helping me keep Ruby's voice real, and for inspiring me, always.

American Airlines Flight 161

I'm not *that* depressed,
considering that this
gigantic silver bullet with wings
is blasting me away from my whole entire life,
away from Lizzie Brody,
my best friend in the world,
away from Ray Johnston,
my first real boyfriend.

Not *that* depressed,
considering I've been kidnapped
by this monstrous steel pterodactyl
and it's flying me all the way to L.A.
to live with my father
who I've never even met
because he's such a scumbag
that he divorced my mother
before I was even born.

I'd say I'm doing *reasonably* well,
considering I'm being dragged
three thousand miles away from all my friends
and my school and my aunt Duffy
and the house I've lived in ever since I was born,
three thousand miles away from my mother,
and my mother's grave,
where she lies in a cold wooden box
under six feet of dirt,
just beginning to rot.

I'm not *that* depressed
considering that I'm trapped
on this jumbo poison dart
shooting me away from everything I love,
and there's this real weird guy
sitting in the seat right behind mine,
who keeps picking his nose
and eating it.

Depressed?
Who? Me?

Aunt Duffy Drove Me to the Airport

And there was a second there
when I actually considered
getting down on my hands and knees
and begging her not to put me on this plane,
begging her not to send me away,
pleading with her to let me stay in Boston
and live with *her* instead.

But Duffy's so nice that I knew she'd say yes
and I knew that that would make me feel
like crawling under a boulder,
because her apartment just has
this one microscopic bedroom

and now that she's finally
got herself a new boyfriend,
the last thing she needs
is to have her fifteen-year-old niece
permanently camped out in her living room,
which is barely even big enough
to fit her couch.

So I contained my urge to grovel.

My Mother Hated Flying

Especially after September 11th.

She used to squeeze my hand so hard
during takeoffs and landings
that she'd cut off my circulation.

She'd screw her eyes closed
and whisper this silly prayer someone taught her once.
Something about manifold divine blessings
being unto the plane or the universe
or *some* hippie-dippy thing like that.

And if there was even
a teensy bit of turbulence—*forget* it.
She'd start apologizing to me
for every mean thing she'd ever said
or done or even *thought* about doing.

This morning,
when the plane was lurching down the runway
and I didn't have Mom's hand to hold,
my heart flung itself up into my throat.
And for a minute there,
I couldn't even breathe.

I didn't know how much
I depended on
being depended on

by her.

Peach Fuzz

When the flight attendant
leans in to ask me
if I'd like something to drink,
and the sun splashes across her face,

I notice
all these tiny little
blond hairs on her cheeks,
and tears rush into my eyes.

My mother had them, too.
I used to tease her about them.
Called it her peach fuzz.
It used to make her laugh.

If I could reach out
and stroke those little hairs
on the flight attendant's face,
without totally freaking her out,

I'd close my eyes
and I'd do it right now.
I'd touch my mother's cheek
one more time.

Maybe You're Wondering About It

But that's just tough.
Because I'm not even going to go *in*
to how she died.

Let's just say she *knew* that she was sick,
that she felt it burrowing,
felt it gnawing at her insides.

But the doctors wouldn't listen.
And when they finally found it,
there was nothing they could do.

Nothing *she* could do.
Nothing *I* could do.
Nothing.

Let's just say
she wasted away into a toothpick,
and leave it at that, okay?

That after a while
she was just a shadow
lying there on her bed.

Oh.
And I guess we can say
that I was holding her hand

when it finally happened.

I Love to Read

But my life better not turn out
to be like one of those hideous books
where the mother dies
and so the girl has to
go live with her absentee father
and he turns out to be
an alcoholic heroin addict
who brutally beats her
and sexually molests her
thereby causing her to become
a bulimic ax murderer.

I love to read,
but I can't stand books like that.

And I flat out refuse
to have one of those lives
that I wouldn't even want
to read about.

And Speaking of Fathers

As soon as I was old enough
to notice that I didn't have one,
I started asking questions.

Like, "Where's my daddy?"
And, "How come Lizzie has a daddy,
but I don't?"

Mom's face would sort of slam shut
and all she'd say was,
"He divorced me before you were born."

If it wasn't for my aunt Duffy
I'd never have even found out
who my father *was*.

My Earliest Memory

I'll probably be lying on a ratty old couch
telling some nosy shrink about this in a few years:

I was just about to turn four.
My aunt Duffy told me she was going to give me
a very special present for my birthday.
She said she was going to take me to see my daddy.
But only if I promised not to tell my mommy.

I remember crossing my heart and hoping to die,
and hurrying to put on my brand-new red sparkle shoes.
Then she popped me into her Volkswagen
and whisked me off to a movie theater.
I figured my dad was going to meet us there.

I remember searching every face in the lobby,
trying to pick him out of the crowd,
while my heart tap-danced against my ribs.
I could hardly wait to show my daddy (*my daddy!*)
those new shoes.

I remember the lights going down, the film coming on,
and there still being no sign of him.
"But where *is* he?" I demanded to know,
on the verge of a major meltdown.

Aunt Duffy put her arm around me,
then pointed to this enormous face up on the movie screen
and said, "There he is, Ruby.

That's your daddy."

My Daddy?!

"But he's too . . . big!" I squeaked.
And it suddenly struck me
that I wasn't going to be able to show him
those new shoes of mine after all.

I burst into tears,
leapt out of my seat and ran up the aisle
with Aunt Duffy right on my heels.

And then we were both in the lobby
and she was crying too
and hugging me so tight my lungs were collapsing
and saying how terribly sorry she was
and going on and on about not being a mom herself
and about being clueless
about how to do things like this the right way.

And I remember feeling
sort of guilty for making her cry.
But then this sudden tsunami of fury crashed over me
and I started shouting at her to just stop crying,
just stop talking,
just stop *everything*—

and bring me back inside the theater
to take another look at my amazing,
colossal,
gigantic

DADDY.

After That It Got to Be a Tradition

Every December, around my birthday,
Aunt Duffy would come to pick me up
and tell my mom that she was
taking me for a girls' day out.

Only what she *really* did
was take me to see
my illustrious father, Whip Logan,
in his latest smash hit.

Can you *believe* that name?
Whip.
It sounds so . . . so *made up*.
How did he ever come up with something that lame?

Whip Logan *is*—*Mr. Millions*.
Whip Logan *is*—*The Seeker*.
Whip Logan *is*—*Sergeant Bennett*.
Whip Logan *is*—*Black and Blue*.

I went to see him faithfully.
Every single year.
But he never came to see me.
Not even once.

That's because Whip Logan *is*—an asshole.

The Year I Turned Nine

It got sort of dicey.

That was when Whip Logan *was—The Final Father*,
a man so evil that he murdered his own children.

Which of course didn't do a whole heck of a lot
for my ability to fall asleep at night.
And it didn't help matters any
that I couldn't even tell my mom
what was keeping me awake,
since Aunt Duffy had drilled it into me
year after year
that if I ever told my mom
about our little trips to the Cineplex,
my mother would murder *her*.

I *knew The Final Father* was only a movie.
But Whip was just too good
at being bad.

Aunt Duffy assured me that my actual father
hadn't actually killed
any actual kids.

She said my father
would never do anything
to hurt me.

Yeah. Right.

Turbulence

*Ladies and gentlemen,
the captain has turned on
the seat belt sign.*

Please return to your seats
and fish your barf bags out
of the seat pockets in front of you

while we prepare
to slam through some
real nasty storm clouds . . .

I think I left my stomach about five miles back.
I wonder if this is what it feels like
to be in an earthquake . . .

What if we get struck by lightning?
What if a huge fist of pissed-off wind
punches one of these pitiful wings right off?

Well, what *if*?
There's a part of me
that wouldn't even mind.

It'd serve my fabulously talented,
deeply neglectful,
Oscar-winning father right.

Window Seat Blues

I have to pee.
So bad.

But the man sitting next to me
looks like a sumo wrestler on steroids.

And just my luck:
he's sound asleep.

Squeezing past him
is definitely not an option.

Maybe if I called the flight attendant
she could have him forklifted.

Only eleven hundred miles
to go.

At least that weirdo behind me
has finally run out of boogers.

In-flight Viewing

Oh. My. God.
I can't believe it.
They're showing that
horrible airplane crash movie!

Just kidding.
Actually,
it's one of those stupid
international spy films.

The kind that has a plot so seriously twisted
that you get a migraine just trying
to keep track of who the good guys are
and who the bad guys are.

At least this one isn't starring Whip Logan
or I might have had to shove open
the emergency exit and take my chances
with my seat cushion flotation device.

Airplane Lunch

They
call
this

chicken?

Dear Lizzie,

    Sorry about writing you this letter on the back of a barf bag, but I'm sitting here on the plane to California and it's the only paper I've got. Besides, it captures my mood perfectly. It's so awful to think that with every word I write, I'm getting farther and farther away from you. And from Aunt Duffy. AND from Ray. How am I going to live without him? I'm so miserable I could puke. But I better not, or I won't be able to send you this letter.

    Don't forget about me. And don't let Ray forget about me either, okay? Keep reminding him how wonderful I am. And tell him to watch out for that disgusting skank, Amber. I just know she's gonna try to move in on him now that I'm gone.

Zillions of kisses from
your pitiful friend in the sky,
Ruby

Ray

He wasn't the first boy I ever kissed.
But he was the first boy I ever *liked* kissing.

All the other ones,
not that there were exactly hundreds,
just seemed to want to ram their tongues
down my throat to distract me from noticing
what their hands were trying to do.

But it was different with Ray.
Right from the start.
When *he* kissed me
it seemed as though he was doing it
because he actually *liked* me.
Not just because he was horny.

It was as if he was trying to show me
how he *felt* about me with those kisses of his.

I sure miss that guy.
I miss the way he always tosses
his black curls off his forehead.
I miss the way he presses his thumb
into my palm when he holds my hand.
I miss the way his chocolate eyes melt right into mine
whenever he smiles at me.

There's a hole in my heart bigger than Texas.
Over which, coincidentally,
we happen to be flying at this very moment.

Three Wishes

I wish Ray was on this plane with me.
I wish we were on our way to Tahiti.
I wish we were the only two passengers
and—

Oh my God!
It's *him!*

He's slipping through the first-class curtain,
passing right by me with this big grin on his face,
motioning for me to meet him at the back of the plane.

I manage to levitate over the sleeping giant next to me,
and float down the aisle right into Ray's arms.

He wraps me into a hug so hot
that I practically burst into flames.

We slip into the bathroom,
and lock the door.
Then, without even saying a word,
we start kissing.

And we kiss and kiss and kiss
until I can feel his kisses running all through me.
And now he's starting to unbutton my shirt and—
that's when I wake up.

No!
I *don't* want any honey-roasted peanuts.

It Figures

The pilot just announced
that there's a breathtaking view
of the Grand Canyon
for the passengers who are seated
on the left side of the aircraft.

Guess which side
I'm sitting on?

Ladies and Gentlemen,
We Are Beginning Our Dissent

Will the passengers in coach class
please return your seat backs and tray tables
to their full upright positions for landing.
And will the passengers in first class
please take a moment
to stow their personal footrests
beneath their seats.

Their personal footrests?!

Oh, and if it's not too much trouble,
would they mind returning
their empty champagne bottles
and caviar buckets
to their personal in-flight servants?

Those first-class passengers
who are still submerged
in their individual hot tubs at this time
should take this opportunity to climb out
in order to allow their geishas
sufficient time to towel them dry.

At this time we must also request
that all the exotic dancers
place their clothes back on their bodies,
and that all masseuses fold up and stow
their portable massage tables

in the massage table bin
located at the rear of the first-class cabin.

Kindly take a moment to hand
your monogrammed cashmere blankets,
your imported goose down pillows,
and your exclusive complimentary
American Airlines Armani bunny slippers
to your personal in-flight butlers
for placement in the overhead compartments.

Thank you for flying with American Airlines.
We hope that all of you,
even the scum
who could only afford coach class,
will have a very pleasant stay here
in the Los Angeles area.

The air quality at the present time
is hideously unhealthy
for all living creatures.

That's L.A. Down There

Lurking under a curtain
of olive brown mist
that's hanging over it
like a threat.

That's L.A. down there,
simmering in that murky smog stew.
But from where *I'm* sitting,
it looks more like

Hell A.

I Didn't Want to Get on This Plane

But now I don't want to get *off* it.

I gather up my stuff in slow motion
and make myself follow
the sumo wrestler down the aisle,
past the flight attendants standing by the cockpit,
grinning and nodding at me
like those bobble-head dogs
that people stick on the
dashboards of their cars.

I force myself to step through
the gaping steel jaw of the doorway,
and inch down the corridor of doom,
balancing on the tightrope
of dirty gray carpet,
painfully aware that every step I take
is leading me
closer and closer

to the sperm donor himself.

There He Is

The
Whip Logan.
In three whole dimensions.

I don't know whether
to ask him for his autograph,
kick him in the balls,

or run.

So I Don't Do Anything

I wish I felt
like racing over to him
and flinging my arms around his neck.

I wish I felt
like telling him I love him
and all is forgiven.

I wish I felt
at least a tiny bit
glad to see him.

Not that *my* feelings
exactly appear to *matter* to him
one way or the other.

He's too busy signing autographs
to even notice
that I've gotten off the plane.

I Watch Whip Logan

Chatting away
with his giggling fans,
scribbling on all their scraps of paper,

and their arms
and their T-shirts
and their whatevers.

I watch him
being so damn friendly
to everyone,

and
I feel—
what *do* I feel?

Nothing.
Nada.
Zip.

Zero.

Uh Oh

He's spotted me.

That nice comfortable
nothing feeling

just morphed into dread.

Here He Comes

The guy from whose
ridiculously famous loins I sprang
is heading straight toward me.

He's walking right up to me,
smiling at *me*
just like he smiled at *Gwyneth Paltrow*,
in that sappy opening scene
from *The Road to Nowhere*.

My real, live, honest-to-goodness dad
is standing here right in front of me
saying, "You must be Ruby."

Who *wrote* this dialogue?

I want to say, "No, duh."
I want to grab him by his collar and scream,
"Where have you been all my life,
you worthless piece of—"

But the words
get all fisted-up in my throat.
So I just nod.

Then his eyes start getting all blurry,
exactly like they did when
he was reunited with Julia Roberts
in that terrible remake of *It's a Wonderful Life*,

and he puts his arm around *my* shoulder,
just like he put his arm around *hers*.

Gag me.

So I duck down,
pretending I have to tie my shoe.
And when I stand back up
he doesn't pull any more of that
arm-around-the-shoulder,
I'm-your-famous-movie-star-father crap again.

At least he's capable of taking a hint.

"Welcome to California!"

He says it like he's rehearsed it.
But he says it like he means it.
Like he really, *really* means it.

Well,
so what if he does?
Because I'm here to tell him
that he can't just ooze out
onto the stage of my life
and *play* my father.

Not after Mom did all the hard work
of teaching me to be a decent human being,
which is something he obviously couldn't have done
even if he'd bothered to try
since he clearly doesn't know the first thing
about being one himself.

I'm here to tell him
that this is going to be
the toughest role he's *ever* had to play.

Suddenly

A billion flashbulbs are exploding all around us
and people are shouting and pushing and shoving
and sticking cameras in our faces
and crowding so close
that it feels like we're in a mosh pit.

"Whip! Whip!" they're calling
from every direction at once.
"Is that your long lost daughter?"
"She looks just like you!"
"Come on, honey, smile for the camera!"
"Hey, Ruby, look over here!"
"Put your arm around her, Whip!"
"Come on, Miss Logan, give us a smile!"

"Damn paparazzi," Whip says under his breath,
and then all of a sudden
these four incredible hulks muscle through the throng
and link arms to make a pathway for Whip and me.
"Thanks, guys," he says as we rush past them.
"We'll see you back at the house."

Then he grabs my hand and starts running
toward the limo that's parked out front.
"I'm so sorry, Ruby," he says,
as we leap inside and it speeds away.
"I hired a look-alike to throw the reporters off the track,
but I guess it didn't work."

Is that *all* you're sorry for, Whip?

It's Creepy Being in a Limo

Because the only other time
I was ever even *in* one
was on the way to Mom's funeral.

And there's a movie star in *this* one.
He's sitting right across from me,
staring at me like *I'm* a movie star.

Only *this* movie star
is my father.
How bizarre is *that*?

He's just sitting here,
staring at me,
trying to catch his breath.

And now his eyes are getting
all disgustingly misty and he's saying,
"You look so much like your mom."

Whoa.
I feel like I'm the co-star
of one of those gruesome soap operas

and the director's going to start shouting "Cut!"
if I don't get a grip
and remember my line.

So I say, "You're a lot *shorter*
than you look on the screen,"
practically spitting the words in his face.

But he just smiles at me,
that same smile that he smiles
in all his movies,

and says,
"I'm sure glad you're here."
Cut. Cut! CUT! *CUT!*

Sightsniffing

Whip tells the chauffeur to turn left on California
and take the Pacific Coast Highway to Sunset.

Then he presses a button on the control panel
and the tinted window floats down.

Across an expanse of strangely duneless sand,
I catch my first glimpse of the Pacific.

A little thrill runs through me.
I've always loved the ocean.

The sound of it, the feel of it . . .
And I guess this one's pretty enough.

But there's something weird about it.
It doesn't smell right.

In fact, it doesn't smell at all.
That's what's wrong.

I fill my lungs with what *should* be sea air.
But I might as well be in Nebraska.

I can't pick up even the vaguest whiff
of seaweed *or* salt.

What kind of an ocean *is* this, anyway?

"You Wanna Stretch Your Legs?"

Whip asks me,
all boyish and perky
and so deeply upbeat
that I want to slug him.

But he doesn't wait for me to answer.
He just tells the chauffeur
to pull into a beach parking lot.
"Let's take off our shoes," he says.

He tears off his $200 Nikes,
leaps out of the limo,
then turns and offers me his hand.
Which I pointedly do not take.

I slip out of my Payless sandals
and suddenly find myself sprinting across
the silky heat of the sand
toward the waves.

I might have been able
to enjoy this moment,
if Whip wasn't prancing along
right next to me.

We don't stop
till our toes are in the water.
"I've always loved the ocean," he says.
"The way it feels, the way it sounds . . ."

And when I hear these words,
something flickers on and off inside of me,
like a tiny flash of lightning.
And I suddenly feel like sobbing.

The tears surge to my eyes,
swelling and stinging like salty waves.
But I don't cry.
I never do anymore.

Not since Mom.
I guess I must have used up
my entire lifetime supply of tears
on the night she died.

Whip Stares Out at the Water

"Maybe we'll spot some dolphins," he says.
And just then,
I see this sleek fin slice through the waves,

this shining fin attached to the back
of a velvety gray creature
that leaps up through the spray.

Suddenly I'm one big goose bump.
I've never seen a dolphin in the ocean before.
Only the one at the aquarium.

And wow!
There's another one. And another.
It's a whole family of them!

Cresting through the waves.
Spinning on their tails.
Like they're putting on a show just for *us*.

And now they're close enough
for me to see the smiles on their faces.
I'm not kidding—they're actually *smiling*!

And then I notice that Whip is, too.
But at *me*.
So I wrestle the smile off my *own* face

and watch *his* fade.

It's a Very Long Driveway

Curving through a forest
of anorexic palm trees,
waving their scrawny necks around
miles above an unnaturally green lawn.

The house finally rolls into view.
It looks like Walt Disney designed it.
Turrets. Balconies. Gables. Flags.

There's even something
that looks sort of like
a drawbridge.

What?
No moat?
Really, Whip.
You're slipping.

I Wonder What Ray Would Think of This Place

It'd probably make him hurl.
He wants to be an architect someday.

Before I left,
he gave me an amazing drawing of a house.
He said he designed it especially for me.

Called it *Ruby's Slipper*,
and said he wished we could live in it
together.

I can't believe that I'm going to be living
three thousand miles away
from that guy.

I can't believe it.
And I can't stand it.

Be It Ever So Humble

Whip guides me through the front door
by my elbow.
(*Does he have to keep touching me?*)

And what I see
makes it awfully hard to keep my eyes
from popping out of their sockets.

The front hall alone
is twice the size
of the house Mom and I lived in.

And the floor twinkles
like something straight out of
an old Fred Astaire movie.

There's a gurgling indoor fishpond
right in the middle of it,
a curved marble staircase on the left,

and off to the right,
a living room roughly the size
of a football field.

Okay.
Maybe I'm exaggerating.
Half a football field.

In the Living Room

I feel like I've just
stumbled through the looking glass
into the Whip Logan Museum.

There's movie posters from all of his films
plastered on the walls,
a framed thank-you letter
from the mayor of New York City,
a plaque from the governor of Someplace-or-other,
and an honorary degree from Yale Drama School.

There's a sculpture of Whip,
an etching of Whip,
a caricature of Whip,
and an enormous oil painting of . . . who else?
Signed by David Hockney.

There's photographs everywhere:
Whip with Madonna.
Whip with Tom Cruise.
Whip with Michael Jordan.
Whip with Steven Spielberg.
Whip with Bill Clinton.

I don't see any
of Whip with the pope,
but I bet there's one around here somewhere.

And in the center of the mantle,
above a fireplace big enough
to rotisserize an elephant,
stands Whip's Oscar,
shimmering,
under the beam of a single spotlight.

Jesus.
If this guy was
any more full of himself,

he'd explode.

He Ushers Me Out of the Room

And up the staircase,
down a hallway
carpeted with a rug so soft
that I sink in past my ankles.

He stops in front of an oak door
and whips it open (pun intended)
to reveal—
my bedroom.

I almost fall over when I see it.
Because it's my dream room.
I mean, I don't think you understand.
It's *literally* the room of my dreams.

And seeing it is this totally
surreal experience because it's the very
same room I described in an essay once
for a contest that won me first prize.

Whoever designed it
must have read my mind.
Because whoever designed it
got it exactly right.

There's the stone fireplace,
the antique stained glass lamps,
and the cozy window seat.
There's even the huge bookcase full of books.

And the canopy bed draped with lace,
heaped so high with comforters and pillows
that you can't even get into it
without stepping up onto a footstool.

Cripes.
It's the room
I've always wanted.
Only I *didn't* want it

here.

A Simple Answer to a Simple Question

"How do you like it?"
Whip suddenly asks,
all bright eyed and bushy tailed,

like he figures I'm going to
fling my arms around his neck and squeal,
"Oh my God! I love it, Daddy!"

So I just yawn.
Then I shrug and say,
"It's okay. I guess."

He's Gone Now

I can finally breathe.

Before he left he said he guessed
I'd probably need some time to settle in
and rest up before dinner.

I need some time all right.
But not to do
what *he* said.

I need some time to call Aunt Duffy
and beg her to send me the money
for a one-way ticket back to Boston.

But when I dial her number,
her phone machine picks up.
And just hearing her voice obliterates me.

I have to hang up fast
to keep myself from leaving her
a truly pathetic message.

Then I call Lizzie.
I call Ray.
But nobody's home.

And neither,
unfortunately,
am I.

Home

I can't believe how much I miss it already.
It wasn't anything like this place.
It was small, but cozy,
overflowing with all kinds of funky stuff
that Mom used to find at flea markets.
And every room was crammed with books.

I guess it was a little bit messy.
Okay. So maybe it was *more*
than a little bit messy.
But it was way comfortable.
Which made it the favorite hangout
for all of my friends.

Especially Lizzie.
Lizzie used to say that she'd give
her right arm to have a house like mine.
And her left one
to have a mother like mine.
And I guess I can understand why.

See, Mom wasn't that corny type
who always had milk and cookies waiting for us
when we'd get there after school.
She was a librarian,
so she didn't usually get home
till just before dinnertime.

But she knew how to listen.
She knew how to laugh.

She knew how to be there when you needed her.
And how to disappear when you didn't.
I loved that about her.
I loved a *lot* of things about her.

Man, sometimes I miss her so much
that I feel as if
I'm burning up with missing her,
as if I'm getting ready to break apart,
to just disintegrate—
like the space shuttle did over Texas.

It Mega-stinks

These days, even when I *want* to cry, I can't.
But that doesn't seem to matter to my face.
Even though no tears come out,
the rims of my eyes turn redder than my hair
and my cheeks get hideously splotchy.

Just like they are right now.
I need to splash some cold water on my face.
So I push open the door
to what I assume must be my bathroom—
and get my mind severely blown.

Boy, I wish Lizzie could see this place.
She would *not* believe it.
I mean there's a sunken tub in here.
And a separate glass shower.
And a sauna. And a steam room.

Oh, and did I forget to mention the bidet?
Lizzie would think it was hysterical.
She'd probably be trying it out right now.
God, I wish she was here.
I wish Aunt Duffy and Ray were here.

What's the point of having
a bathroom that could be featured
on *MTV Cribs*,
when there's no one around I care about
to show it to?

Dinner

I thought there'd be a butler.
Some guy with an English accent
and white gloves, hovering
with assorted silver trays,

lifting off shining domed lids
to reveal steaming . . . steaming . . .
Oh, I don't know.
Steaming crumpets or something.

But it's just Whip.
And me.
Surrounded by
an acre of kitchen.

Just Whip.
And me.
And at least one of every cooking device
known to mankind.

There's even a spatula that automatically
flips pancakes when you press a button.
Which Whip happens to be demonstrating
at this very moment.

He looks like *such* an idiot in that apron,
going on and on about
how his macadamia nut pancakes
are renowned the world over

and about how if he hadn't been an actor
he probably would have been a chef
and about how tangy the oranges from his trees
are at this time of year

and about how he gave his assistant
the weekend off
but I'm going to love him when I meet him
because he's a real hoot

and about how it's fun sometimes
to have breakfast for dinner, isn't it?
And on and on and on and on . . .
until the doorbell rings.

Whip's Up to His Elbows in Pancake Batter

So he sends me to see who it is.
I swing open the door, and practically fall over—
there, standing right in front of me,
is Cameron Diaz.

She grins when she sees my jaw drop,
and explains that she lives next door.
Cameron Diaz is my next-door neighbor?!

Then she says she's so glad to meet me.
She says Whip's told her all about me.
Cameron Diaz knows things about me?!

She says she hates to be a bother
but she was wondering if Whip
could loan her some vanilla extract
for this birthday cake that she's baking for Drew.
Drew Barrymore?!

Then she breezes right past me straight toward the kitchen,
like she's been here a million times before.
Whip lights up when he sees her
and sweeps her into a hug.
She kisses his cheek.

She only stays a minute,
but it's plenty long enough for me to ask
myself the weirdest question of all time:

Is Cameron Diaz going to be my stepmother?

After She Leaves

I take a bite
of Whip's famous pancakes

And they're delicious.
There's no denying it.

But I'd like to ram the whole perfect plateful
right down his throat.

Mom
was a terrible cook.

In My New Bed

There's a full moon tonight,
drifting through the sky
like a sad ghost,

gazing down at me
with these real soft eyes,
as though it understands . . .

How pathetic is that?
The only person on the entire West Coast
that I can actually relate to

is the Man in the Moon.

She's Trying to Get Out!

I can hear her nails
scratching against the inside of the coffin,
hear her thrashing and kicking
and gasping for air that isn't there.

My mother's not dead!
She's been buried alive!
I've got to get her out!
I claw at the heavy lid till my fingers bleed.

I heave my whole weight
against the smooth-as-skin wood,
over and over again.
I can hear her moaning, "Ruby . . . Ruby . . . Ruby . . ."

Suddenly
her hand bursts a hole through the lid
and grabs on to my wrist
with slimy, rotting, horror-movie fingers.

She starts laughing insanely,
trying to pull me down into the coffin with her,
her black nails slicing into my skin—
BEEP! BEEP! BEEP! BEEP!

Thank *God* for alarm clocks.

It's 9:30!

I'm supposed to be ready
to go shopping with Whip
in half an hour!

I catapult out of bed—
and almost shatter my ankle
because I forget how high up I am.

I limp into the shower,
but there's so many dials and high-tech switches
that I can't figure out how the heck any of it works.

So I opt for a bath.
But I must be suffering from a severe case of jet lag,
because I can't even figure out how to close the drain.

Finally,
I just give up,
and wash under my arms.

I've never been in a bathroom before
that made me feel
like such a moron.

I Scramble Down the Stairs

Expecting to see the limo
waiting for us out front,
like a sleek black flashback of Mom's funeral.

But it's nowhere in sight.
Whip leads me over to his five-car garage.
(You heard me right: there's five of 'em.)

Then he asks me
to choose one of the doors,
like I'm a contestant on a quiz show.

I think this
is a real lame thing to be doing,
which I indicate by rolling my eyes,

but I wave my finger
at door number one,
just to get him off my back.

Then he presses a button
and the door swings up,
revealing a cherry red 1952 Chevy Corvette.

How do I know that's what it is?
Because I've always had a thing
for vintage cars.

And this one's in primo condition,
with headlights like sleepy eyes
and a grill like a brace-face grin.

Whip walks over to it and strokes the fender
like he's patting a kitten.
Then he says, "I collect classic cars."

And when I hear this,
that same little flash of lightning
flickers on and off inside of me.

And my cheeks get all splotchy.

They Don't Call It *Labor* Day for Nothing

It's hard work
shopping with a fabulously wealthy father
who keeps buying me everything in sight
to try to make up for an entire lifetime
of world-class neglect.

It's hard work
acting like I really don't want
any of the stuff that he's buying for me,
when the truth is
that I want it very, very much,

only I *don't* want it
because *he's* the one who's buying it,
but I *do* want it because I've always dreamed
of having a computer just *like* this
and all these great clothes and jewelry and shoes.

It's hard work acting like
I could take or leave all this stuff.
But I'd give every bit of it back
before I'd give Whip the satisfaction
of knowing that I'd hate to.

As Soon as Whip's Computer Guy Hooks Up My PC

I check my e-mail.
There's three from Lizzie,
and one from Ray!

My heart starts beating ninety words a minute.
I take a deep breath
and click open his message.

It says that he can't believe
school starts tomorrow.
That he's *so* not ready to hit the books.

It says that he's been thinking of me.
And that he misses me.
And that it sucks that I'm so far away.

"My entire *life* sucks,"
I whisper to the screen,
feeling suddenly and unbearably tragic.

I swear to God.
If Ray walked through my door right now
I'd be so happy to see him

I'd finally let him devirginize me.

Hey Ray,

I dreamt about you on the plane. And when I woke up, and you weren't there, I wanted to jump out the window. But the evil flight attendants wouldn't let me.

The only thing keeping me from drowning myself in Whip Logan's Olympic-size swimming pool is the thought of you coming to visit me at Thanksgiving.

In the meantime, maybe we should try having cybersex. Then again, maybe we shouldn't. Whip's so famous that someone would probably get their hands on a copy of it and publish every word in the *National Enquirer*.

Don't wait until Thanksgiving. Come this weekend. Come right now.

I think you should know that I have a really big bed.

Love and kisses,
Ruby Dooby

The Three E-mails from Lizzie

Dear Ruby,

I can't believe you're gone. It's only been 24 hours, but it seems like light-years. I just spent the entire morning trying to French braid my own hair. The results were *très* ugly. Trust me.

What am I going to *do* without you? I'm suffering from a severe case of Post-traumatic Best Friend Withdrawal.

Love,
Lizzerella

Dear Ruby,

I walked past your house just now and saw a new family moving in. I told them to get the hell out of there. Not really. But I sure wanted to. It made everything seem so final. You're not coming back, are you?

Boo hoo hoo times a zillion,
Lizzette

Dear Ruby,

I ran into Ray at the Gap this afternoon. He said he hasn't been able to sleep since the day you left. And he *looks* it, too, poor guy. We commiserated about you being gone. *And* about the fact that school starts tomorrow. We won't be able to tolerate it without you.

Heart-brokenly yours,
Lizzandra
(President of the We Miss Ruby Club)

Dear Lizard,

School starts *here* tomorrow, too. Sophomore year is going to be unbearable without you and Ray. Whip said my school's called Lakewood, and that it's only a mile and a half away from here. He said it's got a stellar reputation and that he had to pull some major strings to get me in. So I said, "What did you do? Autograph the dean's butt?" At which point he acted like he was astonished, and asked, "How did you know?!" At least I *think* he was acting. I mean I *hope* he was acting. It's hard to tell when that jerk's acting and when he isn't. I frankly don't care if the school is stellar or not. As long as it gets me out of the mansion (you should see this place!) and away from *him*. His ego is bigger than the state of California. It's too awful to even go *into* at the moment.

Give Ray an utterly depressed hug for me.

Miserably yours,
Ruby

P.S. Want to hear something deeply surreal? Cameron Diaz lives next door.

Dear Mom,

How are things in heaven? LOL. Is this like totally sick that I'm writing to you, or *what*? It's not that I actually think your soul's out there fluttering around in cyberspace checking your e-mail, or anything. I mean, I completely *get* that you will never, ever receive this. But I feel like writing to you anyway.

I wish I *believed* in heaven. Because at least then I'd be able to picture you up there with your halo and your wings, flying around with all the other angels, doing good deeds, maybe even watching over me to make sure my life turns out okay. But I *don't* believe in heaven. And mostly, when I try to picture you, all I can see is how grim you looked toward the end, just a pile of bones and see-through skin lying there on the bed.

I hate it, Mom. I hate remembering you looking like that.

I miss you so much. A zillion times more than I even miss Duffy and Lizzie and Ray put together.

Love u 4 ever,
Ruby

Fifteen Minutes of Fame

Just as I'm finishing up
writing that e-mail to my mother,
and I'm about to click off AOL
and drag my miserable bones to bed,

something blinks
on the welcome screen
that catches my eye:
it's a photo of Whip and me at the airport!

The headline says:
WHIP'S WILD CHILD WINGS INTO L.A.
Whip is smiling.
Wild Child is *not*.

My teeth are bared,
my hair's in a frenzy,
and it looks like I'm trying
to claw the eyes out of one of the reporters.

Like whoa . . .
This is *way* too weird for words.
I can't even talk about it right now.
I'm going to bed.

On Deaf (and Dumb) Ears

I definitely don't want
the kids at Lakewood to find out
who my father is.

Which shouldn't be too hard to pull off,
since *his* last name is Logan
and *mine* is Milliken.

So
I tell Whip
that I want to walk myself to school.

But he says,
"Oh, it's no bother at all.
I'd be happy to drive you."

I tell Whip that I really wish he wouldn't.
But he just says,
"Don't be silly. I insist."

And swings open the door
of an incredible 1957 Ford Thunderbird
painted look-at-me green.

The license plate reads: RUBYZDAD.

Grand Entrance

So much for trying to keep
my celebrity-daughter status a secret.

You should have seen the heads swivel
when we walked in here together.
It was like something out of *The Exorcist*.

And I bet you'd barf if you could see
how these women in the administration office
are falling all over themselves right now,
fluttering around Whip like a flock of butterflies on X.

They're telling him how grateful they are
for his generous donation
and how delighted they are that he's volunteered
to be the auctioneer at their second annual Noisy Auction
and how they're sure he'll draw
an even bigger crowd than Hanks did last year.

They're offering him mocha lattes
and Krispy Kreme doughnuts
and some kind of fruit that I've never even *seen* before.
And I'm sitting here right next to him,
crossing my eyes, sticking out my tongue,
and wiggling my ears.
But no one seems to be noticing *me*.

(Okay. So I'm not really doing any of that.
But they wouldn't be noticing.
Even if I was.)

69

Whip Finally Makes Like a Tree

He says he's got to run over to Sony
to do some looping.
Whatever *that* means.

Then he gives my shoulder
this nervous little squeeze,
tells me to have fun,
and exits stage left.

At which point, the dean,
one Ms. Moriarity,
says she's going to take me
on the VIP tour.

Wouldn't
the-*daughter*-of-the-VIP tour
be a tad more accurate?

I Don't Know Why They Call It Lakewood

There's no lake.
And there's no woods.
Just a bunch of Lakeweirds.

Seems like half the girls
are wearing lingerie
instead of dresses.

And the rest of them are wearing jeans
with such major holes in them
that you can see their thongs.

(Only the skanky girls
dressed like that at my old school.
But *here* they all do.)

And most of the boys
look like they're trying to do
Brad Pitt impressions.

These kids have perfect hair.
Perfect teeth. Perfect bodies.
Perfect skin . . .

I can feel a huge zit
blooming on the tip of my nose.
It's flashing on and off like a neon sign.

Electives

I can't believe it.
I just had to choose
between signing up for

Dream Interpretation Through the Ages,
Introduction to Transcendental Meditation,
or The Films of Steven Spielberg.

(But only because The Rhythms of Rap,
The History and Uses of Aromatherapy,
and Organic Farming 101 were already full.)

I chose Dream Interpretation.
So that when I wake up
from this really bad one,

at least I'll be able to interpret it.

Colette

She's deeply,
I mean severely tanned.

Her dress is so short
it's a shirt.

She's got this tattoo of a snake
slithering around her ankle.

And so many parts of her body are pierced
that she jingles when she walks.

I've never met
anyone like her.

I've never even *seen* anyone like her.
Except on MTV.

Dean Moriarity just asked her
to walk me to my first class,

since both of us
are taking Dream Interpretation.

What do you say to a person
with magenta eyes?

I sure hope she's wearing contacts.

Colette Speaks First

"That is *so* last week
it's not even funny,"
she says under her Altoid breath.

I cringe,
sure that she's referring to
my new Kate Spade purse.

But then I realize
she's talking about the dress
on the girl who just wiggled by.

It looks like
a handful of scarves being held together
by a dozen safety pins.

"So *yesterday*," I say.
Colette laughs.
"So one *minute* ago," she says.

Maybe
this will be easier
than I thought.

"You're Whip Logan's Kid, Right?"

Shit.
"I'm afraid so," I say.
"But would you mind
keeping that quiet?"

"Sure, Wild Child," she says with a smirk.
"But everyone who missed you on AOL
saw you drive up with him
in that prehistoric Thunderbird."

Damn.
"But I can relate," she says.
"My *mom's* famous.
And I hate it when people find out who she is.

Because after that
I'm never really sure
if it's *me* they like
or just the fact that *she's* my mother."

"Wow," I say,
instantly bonding with this stranger
in a deep and permanent way.
"That's exactly how *I* feel."

And I find myself telling her
about how strange it was after Mom died,
when everyone found out
that Whip was my father.

How all these kids
suddenly started wanting to hang with me
who had never even acknowledged
my existence on the planet before.

Colette just laughs.
"Well, that won't be a problem at Lakewood.
Half the kids who *go* here
have famous parents."

This is so sick.
But the truth is I'm dying to know
exactly *who* those famous parents are.
Especially Colette's mom.

My Curiosity Is Killing Me

But before I can work up the nerve to ask her,
Colette says, "You know something?
I think your father and my mother
played a married couple in a movie once."

"Then, hey," I say.
"That means we're practically sisters."
"Come on, Sis," she grins.
"We've got a few minutes before class starts.

I'll show you around."
And as we head off,
I casually ask, "What movie *was* it?"
"*McKeever's Will*," she says.

Oh. My. God.
Marissa Shawn's daughter just called me Sis!
(Will you listen to me gushing?
I am *such* a hypocrite.)

Colette's Tour

Well, let's just say
it's a wee bit more extensive
than the tour that the dean took me on.

First,
she shows me the spot behind the gym
where everyone goes
to sneak cigarettes between classes.
(I happen to think smoking's disgusting,
but decide it would be unwise
to divulge this information to my tour guide.)

Next,
she points out a tangled mess of weeds,
maybe twenty feet wide by forty feet long,
and informs me that it's
the organic vegetable garden.

She says there's a patch down at the far end
where a guy named Bing is growing some pot
that's so amazing it's not even funny.
He supposedly has the farming teacher
convinced it's a rare species of mint.
But the word on the street is that it's more like
a don't-ask-don't-tell kind of thing,
because Bing lets the guy "help with the harvest,"
if I know what she *means*.

Then,
before I even have a chance to stop reeling from shock,

she points out the spot
where the coke dealer hangs at lunch,
as though *every* school has one.

After that,
she walks me past the two best places
for making out on campus,
introducing me, along the way,
to an enterprising senior named Lolita
(*Lolita?*)
who sells term papers.

And finally,
she points to a door
that's been painted to look like a starry sky,
behind which our Dream Interpretation class
apparently meets.

Whoa.
Whoa.
If I was a coked-out nympho
stoner cheat who smoked a pack a day,
I'd think I'd died and gone to heaven.

Dream Interpretation

Maybe
this is the norm in Loser Angeles.
Maybe this is just how things are.

Maybe all of the kids in all of the classes
in *all* of the schools around here
have to sit on cushions on the floor
holding hands in a big circle
with their eyes closed

while their teacher burns incense
and strawberry candles
and makes them do deep breathing exercises
and leads them through
these excruciatingly lame things
called visualizations.

Maybe this is just
how things are in Califartia.
Maybe I'll just have to try
to get used to
all this touchy-feely stuff.

Maybe my dream class
is not exactly going to be
my *dream* class.

Then Again, Maybe It Is

Because I have to admit that after Feather
(she actually asked us to call her that!)
finishes doing her stupid visualization thing,
it almost starts getting sort of interesting.
Maybe even a tiny bit fascinating.

She tells us about this psychologist named Fritz Perls
who invented this bizarre technique
for interpreting dreams,
way back in the sixties,
called Gestalt Therapy.

Then she shows us this video
of Fritz doing this therapy on one of his patients.
In the film, the patient is telling Fritz
about a dream that he had the night before,
a dream about being at a train station.

And the patient says that *in* this dream
he's watching all these people climbing up a big staircase.
And then Fritz interrupts him
and tells him that he should *be* the stairs,
that he should talk as if he *is* the stairs.

So the guy looks at Fritz like he thinks
the idea of being the stairs is way idiotic,
but he starts talking anyway.
And he says, "I am the stairs.
People walk on me."

And Fritz says, "Go on."
And so the guy says, "People walk all over me.
People walk all over me to get to the top."
And then he starts bawling like a little kid
and saying that he hadn't realized until this very minute

that he's been letting people walk all over him
his whole entire life,
that he's been letting them use him
and abuse him and it's been making him
angry and resentful and sad.

And I'm watching this film
and I'm really getting into it
because it *is* sort of amazing to see this guy
have this major epiphany about himself
just from one measly dream.

And, I don't know, I guess it feels good
to wrap my mind around some new ideas for a change.
Good to take a break from missing my mom.
And Aunt Duffy. And Lizzie. And Ray.
It even feels good to take a break

from hating Whip.

Multiple Choice Pop Quiz

I will:

A. get used to being expected
   to call all my teachers
   by their first names
   (such as Feather, Troy, Violet,
   and, my personal favorite, Proton)

B. learn not to burst out laughing
   when my math teacher suggests
   that I "take a moment to reflect"
   on how solving the math problem
   made me *feel*

C. adjust to the sound of a gong
   ringing at the beginning
   and the end of each period
   (naturally, they don't have *bells* here,
   that would be too normal)

D. grow accustomed to the fact
   that the cafeteria has *waiters*,
   which is apparently what you have to do
   if you get detention here,
   instead of staying after school

(E.) none of the above

After School - Take One

I step outside—and there's Ray!
Grinning behind the wheel
of his battered blue 1989 Mustang.

He waves.
I melt.
He leaps out of the car
and we run toward each other.

Then he hugs me off my feet.
And I die from joy,
right there in his arms.

After School - Take Two

I step outside—and there's Whip.
Grinning behind the wheel
of a pale yellow 1929 Packard convertible.

He waves.
I freeze.
He leaps out of the car
and runs toward me.

Then he hugs me,
right in front of everyone.
And I shrivel up and die.

(*You* get to guess which one *actually* happened.)

On the Drive Home

Whip plays the concerned parent.
"I thought about you today," he says.
Yeah?
Well, I tried not to think about you.

"I kept wondering
how you were doing," he says.
I bet. Just like you've been wondering
every minute for the last fifteen years, right?

"How was your first day at Lakewood?"
"It was fine."
"How are your teachers?"
"Fine."

"Are the kids nice?"
"They're fine."
"How's the cafeteria food?"
"Fine."

"I just have one more question then," he says.
"Are things fine at Lakewood?"
He cracks up at his own joke
and pretends not to notice that *I* don't.

"I wonder why they call it Lakewood," he says.
"There's no lake and there's no woods."
Jesus H. Christ.
If he does that one more time

I'm going to have to kill him.

85

Aunt Duffy Calls

And all she has to say is,
"Hey, Rube. How are you doing?"
And my eyes threaten
to turn into two gushing faucets.

But it's an idle threat.
Because, of course, they *don't*.
They never do anymore.
My cheeks just do their hideous splotchy thing.

"I've been missing you," she says.
Aunt Duffy's words sound far away,
and so thin, as though she's forcing them out through
a throat that's even tighter than mine is right now.

Sometimes I feel like I'm this geyser
with a cork shoved in its mouth.
Like I'm this overfilled water balloon
that's getting ready to blow . . .

"It's great to hear your voice," I say,
barely managing to swallow back the quiver in my own.
But it isn't great.
It's awful.

Because Aunt Duffy's voice
is an exact replica of my mother's.
And hearing it
splits apart every atom in my body.

What I Say (and Don't Say) to Aunt Duffy to Keep Her from Worrying

Turns out Whip isn't as bad as I thought he'd be.
He's a hundred times worse.

He's got a mega-cool collection
of classic cars in mint condition.
The sole purpose of which
is to draw even more attention to himself.

He took me on an amazing shopping spree
and bought me everything in sight.
But he couldn't buy my love.
'Cause my heart's not for sale.
God. My life's starting to sound like a bad country song.
(Is there such a thing as a good country song?)

Marissa Shawn's daughter and me are like *this*.
Who am I kidding?
She was probably only so nice to me
because she felt sorry for me and my enormous zit.

My bathroom is to *die* for.
And if you don't come out here
and rescue me right now,
I'm going to.

What's that you say?
You're leaving on a six-month-long
archaeological dig with your new boyfriend?

And you won't be reachable
by phone or by e-mail or even by postcard
the whole entire time?
I'm so happy for you!
That's wonderful!
You deserter.
You traitor.
You scum of the universe.
You call yourself an aunt?

I Log on to AOL

And when I see FrankLloydWrong
in my "new mail" box,
my heart starts moshing against my ribs.
That's *Ray's* screen name!

He says that the first day of school sucked.
And that me being in L.A. bites.
Even more than he thought it would.
I like hearing that.

He says, "You're haunting me, girl.
Every night, when I try to fall asleep,
I see your face floating in front of me,
your killer green eyes staring into mine."

I like hearing that, too.
And I like that he says he misses my freckles.
"All three thousand nine hundred
and seventy-one of them."

Ray's so funny.
And *so* far away.
I slide his drawing of *Ruby's Slipper*
out from underneath my pillow,

and hug it to my chest.

I Can't Go *on* Like This

I've got to hear his voice—right *now!*
I grab the phone and punch in Ray's number.
I hear it connect and start to ring.

I can picture the phone in his room,
lying on the nightstand next to his bed.
Ring. Ring. Ring.

Why isn't he picking up?
Maybe he can't get to the phone.
Maybe he's in the shower.

Maybe he's in the shower
and he's completely covered
with suds right now.

Maybe he's even fantasizing
that *I'm* in there *with* him at this very moment
and we're *both* covered with suds.

Ring. Rinnng. RINNNNG.
Come on, Ray, hear the phone.
Hear it.

Now I can picture him cocking his head . . .
listening . . . "Is that the—?"
He hears it!

He grabs a towel
and races to the phone
because somehow he knows it's me.

He just *feels* it.
And he can't wait another second
to talk to me—

"Hello?" I suddenly hear
on the other end of the line.
"Ray!" I cry.

"Nah," the voice says.
"This is his brother.
Ray's not home."

Oh Raymeo, Raymeo,

Wherefore art thou, Raymeo? I tried calling you just now, and you weren't there. ☹ Why weren't you sitting by the phone waiting for my call?! Just kidding. I know you have a life to lead. But I REEEEEALLY wanted to hear your voice. So if you get this e-mail before you go to sleep, CALL ME!

If I don't hear from you, then I'll sneak into your dreams later on and kiss you good night. Maybe I'll even do more than that . . .

Love,
Rubiet

P.S. I liked what you said about my face floating in front of you and about missing my freckles. I miss your freckles, too. All three of them.

Dear Rubinowitz,

Cameron Diaz lives next door?! Whoa! What's she like?

The first day of school wasn't any fun without you. Ray's in my math class. But, unfortunately, Amber is, too. You were so right about her. She's such a slut. She dropped her pencil (accidentally on purpose) right in front of Ray's desk and then leaned way over to pick it up so he could see right down her shirt. But don't worry. I was watching him closely, and he didn't even notice. Trust me.

Oops. GTG. The Evil Stepmom's screaming at me to get started on my homework. She is such a controlling bitch! I can't believe I have to live through ten more months of school before summer vacation. I can't *do* it without you. Come home right this minute!

Love,
Lizanthamum

P.S. I forgot to tell you – when Ms. Welford wasn't looking, Ray passed me a note that said "I miss Ruby." That guy is SOOOOOOO sweet!

P.P.S. Say hello to Cameron for me.

P.P.P.S. Cheer up!

Dear Lizabeth,

Easy for you to say. But I guess I'm not *that* depressed, considering that the biggest tart in the entire galaxy is trying to steal my boyfriend while *I'm* stuck here in Less Angeles, 3000 miles too far away to do a single thing about it.

I'm not *that* depressed, considering that my aunt Duffy's just informed me that she's totally deserting me to go running off with her idiotic new boyfriend and she won't even be able to communicate with me for at least six months.

I'd say I'm doing *reasonably* well, considering that all the girls at my new school look like they just stepped out of the pages of a *Victoria's Secret* catalog, and I have a zit on my nose the size of a giraffe.

I'm not *that* depressed, considering that Whip Logan's ego is listed in the *Guinness Book of World Records*, my best friend lives on the other side of the planet, and my mom's still dead.

Well, maybe I *am* a little depressed.

Love,
Ruby

P.S. I'll say hello to Cameron for *you*, if you'll kill Amber for *me*.

Dear Mom,

How are things in the after life? *Is* there an after life? LOL.

I got one of those "Returned mail: Host unknown" e-mails from AOL after I wrote you the first time. It said that your address had "permanent fatal errors." Ha! *I'll* say. That permanently fatal part is what I hate the most about death.

Sometimes, I still can't believe that you're never coming back.

Love u 4 ever,
Ruby

I Had My Recurring Dream Again Last Night

The same dream I've been having
ever since I can remember.
It's the one where I'm about two years old
and I'm at the Franklin Park Zoo,
holding hands with this real tall man.
I'm not exactly sure who he is.
But I'm holding this man's hand,
and it feels nice and warm and dry.

We're standing in front of the monkey cage,
watching all these funny red monkeys
eating bananas and swinging from branches
like tiny, furry acrobats,
and I'm feeling like I could
just stand here watching these monkeys,
holding this man's nice, warm, dry hand
forever.

And at this point in the dream,
the smallest monkey always opens its mouth
and lets out a howl,
a howl louder than any howl could possibly be,
a howl that slices through me like a chain saw.
And all the other monkeys start howling too,
and they howl and howl and howl,
until I feel like I'll explode with the sound.

And I try to run away,
but my legs are paralyzed.

So I just stand there,
letting the howls rip through me.
And that's when the tall man reaches down,
scoops me up in his arms,
and whispers, "I'll keep you safe."

He whisks me away from the earsplitting noise,
to a quiet place.
And that's when I always put one of my chubby
two-year-old hands on each of his cheeks
and press my forehead against his.
It feels nice and warm and dry.
Just like his hand.

And then I wake up.

So, Fritz

What do you think I should be?

The monkey?
The man?
The nice, warm, dry hand?
The cage?
The howl?

Or the banana?

Doing Gestalt Therapy on Myself Seems So Lame

But, heck.
I wouldn't mind having
an epiphany of my very own.
So I guess I'll try *being* the banana.
I feel like an absolute idiot doing this,
but here goes:

I am the banana.

I am the banana
and the monkey is eating me.
The monkey is devouring me,
bite by bite.
I am disappearing
into the stomach of the monkey.

I am disappearing.

I am being digested.
I am turning into shit.
My *life* is turning into shit.

My life is shitty?
Geez, what's *that* supposed to be?
An epoophany?

Tell me something I *don't* know.

It's the Second Day of School

And Whip *still* wouldn't let me walk there.

Even though I practically
got down on my hands and knees
and begged him.

He just popped me into this
1938 Pontiac woody station wagon
with these perfect birch panels,

and said, "Aw, come on, Ruby.
Indulge me . . .
I've been missing out on doing this for years."

As if I could care
about what *he's*
been missing out on.

The Next Few Days Just Sort of Blur By

Like I'm riding on a train
through the pouring rain
trying to see out the window
wearing someone else's glasses.

Every day, when I get home after school,
the house is crawling with strangers.
And Whip insists on introducing me
to every last one of them.

He puts his arm around my shoulder
and says, "I'd like you to meet my daughter."
His daughter, he says,
like he *owns* me.

I meet Whip's tailor,
Whip's interior decorator,
Whip's chiropractor,
and Whip's psychic.

I meet his lawyer, his agent,
his masseuse, his business manager,
his business manager's masseuse,
and his agent's lawyer.

I meet his broker, his gardener,
his housekeeper, his homeopath,
his acupuncturist, his manicurist,
and his violinist.

101

Okay.
He doesn't really have a violinist.
I was just messing with you.
But he *does* have all those other people.

It apparently takes
half the population of Lost Angeles
to keep Whip Logan functioning.
This guy's *entourage* has an entourage.

And Most of Them Seem Like Kiss-ass Jerks

But this one guy named Max is okay.
Whip introduces him as his assistant
slash personal trainer
slash all-round lifesaver.

He's the only one
out of that whole pack of hangers-on
who doesn't tiptoe around Whip
like he's breakable or something.

And he actually seems interested
in getting to know me.
Even asks me how I like California.
And if I miss being back east.

He's the only one
out of all of them
who gives my hand this little squeeze
and says he's so sorry about my mother.

The only one who offers to pulverize Whip
if he gives me the slightest bit of trouble.
He's just kidding,
but it still makes me feel good.

He's this big bearded bruiser of a guy,
with a voice more gravelly than Hagrid's,
and that name that makes him sound like he
sits around all day playing poker and smoking cigars.
But he can't fool *me*—I know he's gay.

How Do I Know?

My gaydar.
I was born with it.
It's my sixth sense.
I think I inherited it from my mother.

Sometimes I know a guy's gay
even before *he* does.
It's just this ability I have.
My mom had it, too.

She used to say it didn't have anything to do
with how they held their tea cups
or their taste in music
or things like that.

She just *knew*.
It was something else,
she used to say.
Something she could *smell*.

I guess by now you've figured out
that Mom was prejudiced against gays.
Of course, she never would have admitted it.
I even hate to admit it *about* her.

But she definitely was.
How did I know?
Let's just say
it was something I could smell.

I Wonder If Max is Trying to Hide It

Or if that's just how he is.
Not all gay guys are swishy, you know.
Not all of them lisp.
That's just a myth.

When we're alone,
I ask him if he likes Streisand,
to let him know
that I know he's gay.

He says he prefers Eminem.
Says the guy's a true poet.
Which is exactly how *I* feel,
actually.

He says he doesn't have much of a knack
for interior decorating either,
in case I was wondering.
And then he grins at me, and winks.

Whip's such a lug.
I bet he doesn't even realize Max is gay.
I'd sure like to see the look on that
famous macho face of his when he finds out.

But Max's
little secret
is safe
with me.

Dear Mom,

How are things in the casket? Not too damp, I hope. ☺

I've met the coolest guy. He works for He-who-shall-not-be-mentioned. His name is Max. I'm not going to tell you about him though, because you wouldn't approve. And no, it's not a love thing. So you don't have to worry about any hanky-panky . . . Speaking of which, you aren't like *all-knowing* now, or anything, are you? I mean, you can't see every move I make down here in Hollyweird can you? If so, quit snooping and get a life. JK.

Love u 4 ever,
Ruby

My Phone Rings

I pounce on it.
"Hey, Rubinski," a raspy,
Marge Simpson-esque voice says.
"How the heck *are* you?"

It's Lizzie calling!
Good old Lizini,
darling Lizabella,
dearest most wonderful Lizeetheus!

(Okay. So maybe I'm overdoing it.
But until I heard her voice,
I didn't realize how much
I'd been *missing* it.)

Lizzie tells me
how miserable she is without me
and how miserable Ray is without me
and about all of Amber's latest tacky moves.

And I tell Lizzie
about Lakewood and about Max
and about Colette and about
what a pitiful excuse for a father Whip is.

I even tell her
about those e-mails
that I've been sending
to a certain dead mother.

"Do you think I should seek
professional help?" I ask her.
"Most definitely," she rasps.
"Dr. Lizzie Freudy, at your service."

Then she laughs,
that perfect rumbly laugh of hers,
and I miss her so much
I can hardly bear it.

But Suddenly She Says She's Got to Go

"Because The Evil Stepmom is suffering from
severe Pre-menopausal Hormonal
Haywire Disorder," she explains.

"And trust me, if I don't quit talking to you
and go help her in the kitchen *right now*,
my ass is grass."

That's not hard to believe.
I can hear her stepmom howling at her
louder than the monkeys in my recurring dream.

So we say quick good-byes and hang up.
I feel a pang in my stomach,
like someone just handed me some Sour Skittles

and then grabbed them away again
before I even had a chance
to pop a single one of them into my mouth.

I just sit there,
staring at the silent phone in my hand.
Then I do the only sensible thing:

I call up Ray.

He Answers the Phone

When he hears my voice, he almost shouts,
"Whoa! Is this really *you*, babe?"
And I practically swoon.

It's as though I can *feel* his voice,
feel his words brushing against my cheek,
his lips brushing against my ear,
his tongue brushing across my . . .

"Dooby?" he says. "You still there?"
And I realize I haven't been listening
to a word he's been saying.

"I'm still here," I say.
"But I wish
I was *there*."

"How's the Weather in Tinsel Town?" He Asks

"*What* weather?" I say.
"It's raining cats and dogs *here*," he says.
"Listen."

I hear the sound
of a window being shoved up.
Then I hear the rain.

So clearly—like it's coming down
right outside *my* window.
My eyes threaten a storm of their own.

"Remember that night last summer
when we went to see the movie
about the hurricane?" I say.

"And when we went outside afterward,
it was so funny, because it was pouring
and we felt like we were *in* the movie?"

"How could I for*get* it, babe?" he says.
And for a few seconds
we share a delicious silence,

remembering together
how he threw his coat over our heads and
we ran down the sidewalk joined at the hip,

and then he pulled me under an awning,
and we kissed and kissed and kissed
while lightning strobed the sky.

"Mmmm," he says. "That was the night
that your dress shrunk two sizes.
Right while you were *wearing* it!"

"I dreamt about that night last night," I say.
"Only in my dream,
we did *more* than kiss . . ."

Then he murmurs
in this real husky voice,
"You're driving me crazy, woman . . ."

"God," I say.
"I wish Thanksgiving was tomorrow."
"I wish it was right *now*," he whispers.

But Thanksgiving
is still two whole months away.
How am I going to survive until then?

Midnight Shock

I tiptoe down
to the kitchen

to try to sublimate my sexual frustration
with a Häagen-Dazs bar—

and find Max sitting at the kitchen table.
In his pajamas!

"What are *you* doing here?!" I ask.
"I live here," he says.

"Right in the same house with us?" I say.
"Yep. This very one."

"Where's your room?"
"Just behind that door over there."

"In the assistant slash personal trainer
slash all-round lifesaver's quarters?" I ask.

"You guessed it," he says.
"My homie!" I say.

And we slap each other five.

Blank Book

Feather just gave every kid
in my Dream Interpretation class
a blank book to write in.
She called them dream journals
and said that our homework
is to record our dreams in them
every morning when we wake up.

I love books.
But blank books scare me.
It's like all those empty white pages
are just lying there
waiting to pounce
on my deepest innermost feelings
and expose them to the entire world.

Besides.
There's no way I'd ever put
a mega-steamy dream
like the one I had last night,
about Ray and me in the rain and all that,
down on *paper.*
But as far as homework assignments go—

this one's gonna be a dream.

Then Again

Maybe it's not.
Because the most awful thing has happened:
ever since Feather said
that we had to record our dreams,
I haven't been able to remember a single one.

Every morning we sit in a circle,
and all the other kids open up their journals
and read their dreams aloud
so that Feather can help them
to interpret them.

When it's my turn, I just blush and mumble,
"Sorry. I still couldn't remember any."
At which point, Feather smiles sweetly
and says something very sixties,
like "go with the flow" or "let it be."

But it's been almost two weeks now,
and that smile of hers is starting to look
a little tight around the edges.
I'm afraid she's beginning to suspect
that I'm a shirker . . .

Heck.
Is it my fault my unconscious
is so unconscious?

And Things Haven't Gone So Well with Colette Either

In the beginning,
I thought we were really gonna hit it off,
like we did when she gave me
her guided tour of the campus.

For the first few days of school,
she kept calling me Sis
whenever she saw me in dream class.

And when Feather made us sit
in that dumb circle and close our eyes,
Colette and I secretly kept ours open
and crossed them at each other.

(*Hers,* by the way,
are a different color every day.
She says tinted contacts are her trademark.)

Once, she even offered
to loan me one of her dreams,
so Feather wouldn't think
I was such a slacker.

There were even some days after school
when Colette would jingle over to me
and invite me to go to Poquito Mas for tacos,
with her and Crystal and Bette and Madison,
like I was a certified member of the in crowd.

But I always had to say that I couldn't.
Because Whip was picking me up.
And after I turned her down a few times,
she stopped asking.

Lately,
when she sees me in class or around school,
she acts like she can't quite place me.
As though she knows she's met me before,

only she just can't remember where.

A Typical Morning in the Life of Me

6:45	turn off alarm clock
6:46	try to remember dreams
6:48	fail to remember dreams
6:49	curse loudly and beat pillow with fists
7:00	drag self out of bed
7:01	brush teeth, take shower, get dressed
7:25	try to make hair look presentable
7:29	give up on making hair look presentable
7:30	curse loudly and beat hair with brush
7:35	eat breakfast with Whip, while fending off his annoyingly perky chatter
7:50	try to convince Whip to let me walk to school
8:00	fail to convince Whip to let me walk to school
8:01	curse inwardly and contain urge to beat Whip over head with hundred-pound backpack
8:02	stomp out of kitchen
8:03	toss self into car and slam door
8:04	say something snotty to Whip about not being allowed to walk to school
8:05	get even more pissed because he doesn't react
8:10	arrive at Lakewood
8:11	get out of car, slam door, don't look back

Lakewood Daze

Some days,
when Madison sees me in the hall,
she smiles at me and says, "What's up?"
And Crystal flashes me the peace sign
and her BriteSmile grin.

Some days,
during herstory class,
Bette keeps passing me these
little slips of paper
with yo mama jokes written on them.

And I can't help laughing,
even though those kind of jokes
aren't quite as funny somehow
when yo *own* mama
is dead.

Some days,
kids I don't even know say hello to me.
And the guy who everyone says
is Harrison Ford's love child,
actually remembers my name.

Some days,
instead of completely ignoring me,
Colette bats her yellow
(or aqua or orange or whatever) eyes at me,
and even says, "Hey."

Those are the days
it almost starts seeming
like maybe there's a pretty good chance
that I might even be able to fit *in* here.
Eventually.

But most days,
I wander around Lakewood feeling invisible.
Like I'm just a speck of dust
floating in the air
that can only be seen

when a shaft of light hits it.

A Typical Rest of the Day in the Life of Me

3:30   toss self into car with Whip

3:32   say something snotty about not being allowed to walk home from school

3:38   arrive home, leap from car, slam door, don't look back

3:45   wade though hordes of hanger-onners to give friendly greeting to Max, especially friendly if Whip is present to witness

3:46   decline Whip's offer for afternoon snack

3:48   retire to bedroom and start blasting Eminem CDs

3:50   log on to get update on Amber from Liz and write flirty e-mail to Ray, or if lucky, get phone call or IM from one or both of above

4:50   put on bikini, grab book, head down to pool

5:00   immerse self in book, or hang with Max, if he's around

5:30   immerse self in pool - laps, if alone, Marco Polo, if with Max

6:00   beg Max to have supper with us so I won't have to be alone with You Know Who

6:02   pummel Max when he says he'd love to, but he thinks it would be best if Whip and I had some time alone together because he's actually a pretty great guy once you get to know him

6:15   eat dinner with Whip while fending off his annoyingly perky chatter

6:30   say something snotty about size of Whip's ego

6:31   note hurt expression on Whip's face

6:35	start thinking about apologizing to Whip
6:36	stop thinking about apologizing to Whip
6:50	excuse self from table and go to room
6:51	start thinking about how much I miss Mom
6:55	log on and write e-mail to her
7:05	curse loudly and beat self-pitying thoughts about being motherless child out of head
7:10	begin homework
10:15	finish homework
10:30	decline offer for midnight snack with Whip
10:45	beg unconscious mind for a dream . . .
6:45	. . . turn off alarm clock
6:46	try to remember dreams
6:48	fail to remember dreams
6:49	curse loudly and beat pillow with fists

Hey Rubinowski,

Still e-mailing your dead mom? You are *so* in denial. But go for it, girl. You gotta work your way through those five stages of grief. Da soona da betta.

And speaking of grief, Ray and I sat together at lunch today and spent the whole entire time talking about how much we missed you. Amber positioned herself at the table right across from ours and kept her legs spread so far apart that you could see her thong. But Ray didn't even glance her way. Trust me. Not even when she knocked her lunch tray onto the floor and made this big squealy commotion to try to get his attention. He just kept on telling me about how he can hardly wait to visit you at Thanksgiving. And *I* can hardly wait to hear about it when he *does*. It's gonna be so *hot*!

Just hang on. It'll be turkey time before you know it.

Love,
Lizziola

Dear Lizzorama,

I'll try. But I miss him like crazy. And I miss you, too. Things really stink here. Every morning for like the past month I've begged Whip to let me walk to school. But he refuses. He apparently thinks I'm only saying I want to walk because I don't want to be a nuisance to him. He keeps telling me that he *wants* to drive me to school. That it's no trouble at all. That he looks *forward* to picking me up at the end of the day.

I've tried explaining that I *like* to walk. That I need the exercise. That he's ruining any chance I have at a decent social life. I've even tried threatening to get carsick all over his 1954 Buick Wildcat's original red leather upholstery. But it just goes right in one of his fabulously famous ears, and out the other.

I hate him. And I hate my life. Help!!!

Love,
Ruby

P.S. Hey. I said hello to Cameron for *you*. But you didn't kill Amber for *me*. How come she's still alive? Couldn't you at least maim her? I thought you were my friend . . .

Two Against One

I tell Max
it's causing me unendurable agony
how Whip keeps insisting on
driving me to and from school every day.

A few minutes later,
I overhear Max telling Whip
that he ought to let me walk
and stop treating me like a child.

Whip tells Max
I *am* a child
and that the world is crawling with perverts
and he'll be worried sick if he lets me walk.

Max tells Whip
he'll just have to live with that
because I'm fifteen years old and
he's behaving like an overprotective idiot.

Then Whip tells Max
he's fired.
But it's pretty obvious
that he doesn't mean it.

Because a few minutes later,
Whip slips into my room and tells me
that from now on
I can walk.

But only if I promise
not to talk to any strangers.
I say, "Okay. But is it all right
if I take candy from them?"

Whip laughs
and draws an imaginary number one in the air,
as though my stunningly witty remark
just scored me a point or something.

I find this deeply irritating
because I was *trying* to be snotty.
Not clever.
And he didn't even notice.

Thanking Max

I tell Max I'm going to give him
my first-born child.
He grins and says
that won't be necessary.

I tell him he's the best friend
a girl could ever hope to have.
He says,
"Yeah. I know."

I tell him he reminds me
of my aunt Duffy.
He says,
"Is it the beard?"

"No," I say.
"It's the big heart."
Which I know sounds totally corny,
but I can't help it, it just pops out.

And suddenly I find myself
telling him all about how much I miss Duff,
and about how I can't even call her
or write to her or anything

because she's off on that endless dig
with that idiotic archaeologist of hers,
and about how severely pissed off I am at her
for disappearing right when I need her most.

"That woman sounds like *such* a bitch!"
he says, in this real swishy voice.
"How dare you compare me
to that nasty, self-centered slut?!"

Which cracks us both up.
And after this,
whenever we're alone,
I call him Aunt Max.

Walking to School for the First Time

Someone's written
"Lotus loves River"
into the cement on the sidewalk.

A Barbie-doll-sprung-to-life
is jogging toward me
screaming hideous things into a cell phone.

And here comes Ken on Rollerblades,
the gold ring in his navel
sparking with sunlight.

Cameron just zipped by on a shiny yellow bike,
gave me a friendly wave,
and shouted out, "Hey, Ruby!"

And I could swear
I just saw Johnny Depp
behind the wheel of that silver Porsche.

If I had a dog named Toto,
I think you can guess
what I'd be saying to him right about now.

Ignorance of the Law

I'm crossing Sunset Boulevard,
dodging all the Mercedes and Jaguars,
when I hear the thin scream of a siren.

I turn to look.
A police car's coming up fast,
flashing its liquid lights.

I glance around to see who they're after
and suddenly realize who they're after
is *me*.

The cop leaps out looking like a model—
dark glasses, deep tan,
dangerously white teeth.

"You weren't in the crosswalk," he says,
seductively raising one eyebrow.
Then he presses something into my hand.

Oh.
My.
God.

I just got a ticket for crossing the street.

Which, of Course, Made Me Late to School

So I'm sprinting across the Lakewood lawn,
trying to get to my dream class
before the first period gong rings,

when I notice
at least a dozen other kids
racing to *their* classes, too.

But all of *them*
are using the sidewalk
that borders the grass.

There aren't any signs posted
warning us to keep off of it.
So what's up with all these airheads?

Didn't anyone ever tell them
that the shortest distance between two points
is a straight line?

Then suddenly
I'm surrounded by an army of sprinklers,
hissing up from the ground all around me.

And,
in one split second—
my T-shirt reveals all.

I Slosh the Rest of the Way to Class

And drip into the back of the room
with my arms folded tightly across my chest,
willing myself to be invisible.

But it must not be working.
Because Colette spots me.
Instantly.

And instead of
looking right through me,
like she usually does,

instead of
doing something way juvenile
like bursting out laughing,

instead of pointing at me and shouting out,
"Looks like Wild Child's the winner
of our wet T-shirt contest,"

she just slinks over to me
with her sequined black leather jacket
and helps me slip into it,

before anyone even
notices the fact
that I'm not wearing a bra.

After Class

When I try to express
my undying gratitude,
Colette just grins
and puts her multi-ringed finger
up to my lips to shush me, saying,
"That's what sisters are for, right?"

"What do you mean, sisters?"
I want to say.
"You've been pretending I don't exist
for weeks now."
But I just nod and smile,
wondering why she's being so suddenly nice.

And it's like she can read my mind
or something, because she says,
"Same thing happened to me once.
Only no one loaned me their jacket.
My nipples became legendary.
It wasn't even funny how mortified I was."

Then she jingles toward the door,
glancing back at me with her pink eyes,
(yep—today they're pink)
and says, "Why don't you just
keep it till lunch
and give it back to me then?"

So That's Exactly What I Do

But for some unknown reason,
all morning long
*every*one who sees me wearing it
feels compelled to comment on it.

Real intelligent comments, like this one:
"Omigod!
Where'd you get that jacket?
Colette has one *exactly* like it."

And: "Has Colette seen that jacket?
She thought *hers*
was the only one in the Universe.
She'll die when she sees *yours*."

And *this* deeply charming remark,
uttered by a guy in my herstory class:
"Hey. You're wearing Colette's jacket.
Does that mean you two lesbos are in love?"

"No," I say under my breath,
"It means you're a pig."
Sheesh. I'm starting to think
it might just have been easier

to cope with having legendary nipples.

I'm Sitting by Myself in the Cafeteria Reading a Book (Like I Do *Every* Day at Lunch)

When Colette comes over to me.
I hand her her jacket and thank her again.
She shrugs and says, "No problemo."
Then she plops down right across from me,
as though she eats with me
all the time.

"What are you reading?" she asks.
"It's called *Stuck in Neutral*," I say.
"What's it about?"
"Oh, this kid who has cerebral palsy," I say.
"And his father's thinking about killing him
to put him out of his misery."

"I can *so* relate to that," she says.
"Just this morning I was thinking about
killing my *mom*—to put *me* out of *my* misery.
My mother can be a monster pain in the butt."
"Yeah," I say.
"But at least you *have* a mother."

At which point,
Colette turns a deeper shade of pink
than the contacts she's wearing.
"Oh. Yeah. Sorry. Oops," she says.
Jesus. What is my problem?
Why did I have to say that?

A silence drifts down over us
and hangs in the air like smog.
Then Colette leaps up,
says, "Later,"
and jingles over to the table by the window,
where Bette and Madison and Crystal are sitting.

I sure blew *that*.

After the Last Gong of the Day

I cram my books into my backpack,
head out into the hall,
and almost get mowed down
by Colette and her friends,
who're high-fiving each other
and laughing hysterically about something.

As they disappear around the corner,
it crosses my mind
that Whip isn't coming to pick me up.
And that for the first time
since the beginning of the school year
I could actually *go* to Poquito Mas with them.

If only they'd ask me.

I'm Walking Home from School

When I glance up and almost scream:
there's Whip's face—
ten stories tall!

He's grinning down at me from a billboard
that's been painted on the side of
an office building near Tower Records.

I try to look past him,
at the sky or the clouds . . .
Only there *aren't* any clouds.

There never *are* in L.A.
I don't think I've seen a single cloud
since I got to Hollywood.

I didn't know
how much I *liked* them
till now.

I miss seeing them
dotting the air like lazy lambs
grazing on fields of blue grass.

I miss watching them
rush past the rooftops
like ghosts in a hurry to get home.

I miss trying to find funny faces in them,
like I used to
with Mom.

No Clouds

No rain.
No hail.

No fog.
No nothing.

Every day's hotter
than the day before.

October's here.
But leaves don't fall.

There isn't any weather
at all.

No rain.
No hail.

No fun.
No friends.

No clouds.
No fog.

Just smog.

I Hear a Sort of Twisting Rustling Sound

It's coming from overhead.
I glance up just in time
to see this gigantic palm frond
plummeting toward the ground
like a suicidal broom.

It crashes down
onto the hood of a BMW
that's parked on the street
only a few feet away from me,
and leaves a nasty dent.

Man.
Back east,
if you get hit on the head
by a falling leaf,
you might not even notice.

Out here,
you could end up with brain damage.

As I Head Up the Driveway

I'm thinking that even if
these stupid shredded fronds,
clacketting together in the tops
of all these needle-necked palms,

were to turn orange and gold
and shimmering crimson rose
and suddenly drop to the ground,
what good would it do me?

I still wouldn't be able
to rake them up into huge soft piles
like I used to rake
the maple leaves back home.

And even if I could,
I wouldn't exactly be able
to jump into a pile of palm fronds
without getting all cut up, now would I?

I know fifteen
is way too old
to jump in the leaves
and I haven't actually done it in years.

The truth is,
I wouldn't be caught dead jumping in the leaves *now*.
But I guess I liked knowing that they were there.
Just in case.

Trudging Through Whip's Pathetic Palm Forest

I'm suddenly decked
by this major wave of nostalgia
for the maple tree in my front yard back home.

I miss its knotty old arms,
and that lap-like spot
between its two lowest branches,

such an easy climb up,
as though it had grown like that on purpose
just for me.

I read *The Whipping Boy* sitting in that tree.
I read *A Wrinkle in Time* there.
And *Tuck Everlasting*.

I read *To Kill a Mockingbird*
in that maple.
And every word Richard Peck ever wrote.

I read *Speak*
and *Hard Love* and *Hope Was Here*
in those branches.

And Mom and I
were sitting up there
when she read me *Charlotte's Web*.

That was *some* tree.

Oh, *Great*

Whip's standing out in front of the house
waiting for me.
And when he sees me,
he shouts out my name and starts
trotting down the driveway toward me
like that puppy I had when I was seven,
who used to get so excited when I got home from school
that he'd pee all over me.

"Boy, am I glad to see you," Whip says.
"If you hadn't shown up in another couple of minutes,
I was going to get a posse together."

A posse?

Now, I don't usually think of myself
as a particularly *mean* person,
but suddenly my mouth flies open
and the words come shooting out like arrows.
"What I can't understand, Whip,
is why you're so worried about me *now*,
when you haven't given a shit about me
for the last fifteen years."

Whip's tail suddenly stops wagging.
"That's not how it was. I've been wanting to explain—"
"I don't care *what* you've been wanting," I say.
And I brush right past him,

into the house.

When I Get Upstairs to My Room

I find a package lying on my bed.
It's from Lizzie!

I rip it open.
And instantly go mega-splotchy:
it's filled with fiery red maple leaves.
They're from my old tree, her note says.
My old tree!

But the thing is,
she's ironed them flat
between two sheets of wax paper.
"So they'll last," she says.

I try to pull the sheets apart,
but they're all melted together.

That damn wax paper.
It makes it impossible to smell them.
Impossible to feel them.
Impossible.

I know Lizzie meant well,
but there's just something so awful about those leaves,
something so completely pathetic
about the fact that they're the only
real bit of fall I'll see this season.

I crumple them up
and fling them into the wastebasket.

Dear Lizistrata,

Your care package just arrived. Thanks SOOOOOO much for the maple leaves. They almost made me cry.

Wistfully yours,
Ruby

P.S. Ray's not succumbing to Amber's scuzzy charms, is he? Keep reminding him how wonderful I am.

P.P.S. *Am* I wonderful? I'm feeling insecure today . . .

I'm in the Middle of Writing
Yet Another E-mail to My Late Mom

Demanding to know why on earth
she ever even married He-who-shall-not-be-mentioned
in the *first* place,
when there's a tap at my door.

I yank it open, hoping it's Max.
But, naturally, it's the scumdad,
looking all hangdog and pitiful.
Sort of like he did in *Sing to the Wind*,
in that scene where he finds out
that Meg Ryan is dumping him
for his best friend.

He says that he knows I'm angry.
And that he doesn't blame me in the slightest.
And that if he was me,
he'd feel exactly the same way.
But that he wishes I'd give him a chance to explain
why he and my mother
had to break up all those years ago.

I stand here for a minute,
staring into his pathetically pleading eyes,
then I slam the door right in his face,
just liked he slammed the door in mine

before I was even born.

And I've Got to Admit:

It feels grrreat!

But a little while later,
I glance out the window
and see Whip sitting in the gazebo,
slowly turning the pages of a big scrapbook.

He must be trying to cheer himself up
by reliving his glorious rise
to fame and fortune.
Figures.

Then Max comes over
and sits down next to him.
They look through a few pages of the book
together.

Does Whip
have something in his eye?
Or is that a *tear*
he's swiping at?

Geez.
I hope it's not a tear.
Oh, *geez*.
Max just handed him a Kleenex.

Hey, Wait a Minute

Answer me this:

If Whip was planning
on getting all weepy,
how come he just happened
to choose to do it
in a spot so clearly visible
from my bedroom window?

I'm only asking you this because
Lizzie must have spent at least a decade
trying to explain to me
what passive-aggressive means.
But I could never get it through
my thick skull.

Until today.

But Even So

Maybe I ought to cut the guy some slack.
I mean the only real trouble he's given me
since I've been out here
is that not-letting-me-walk-to-school thing.

I suppose
I ought to be able
to just let bygones be whatevers.
But grudges Я me.

Forgiving people was hard for Mom, too.
She never forgave Whip, that's for sure.
She never even had another boyfriend,
after him.

She swore off love. Swore off men.
Said none of them were to be trusted.
Which made things pretty sticky
when I started hanging with Ray.

Mom was all *over* me about him.
How did I know he really liked me?
How did I know he wasn't just using me?
How did I know he wouldn't break my heart?

I had to be home by eleven o'clock.
And we could never *ever* be alone together,
in *his* house *or* mine.
Not even in the kitchen.

But I guess Mom forgot
just how alone
and just how together
you can be

in a car.

The Night Before I Left for Califeelia

Ray and I drove out to the reservoir
and sat together in his Mustang,
listening to the rain whisper on the roof,
watching it ripple in melting ribbons
down the windshield.

Then we drifted
deep into the backseat,
drew the curtains of steam down
over the windows,
and kissed.

When our tongues touched,
it felt like chocolate melting . . .
Ray kept on trying to reach around
and undo my bra strap.
But he couldn't quite manage it.

Which was a lucky thing for me.
Because I might have fainted
if there hadn't been a layer of lace
between his fingers and my skin.
If that's what second base feels like,

third base must *really* be something.

There's Another Tap at My Door

I open it a crack.
This time it *is* Max.
And I'm way relieved to see him.

But I can feel my cheeks catching fire.
Whip probably told him about
how I slammed the door in his face.

Max sits down
on the edge of my bed.
"Want to talk about it?" he asks.

Sweet.
Whip *did* tell him.
I shake my head no.

"Want me to eat dinner with you guys tonight?" he asks.
"Oh, *would* you?" I say,
flinging my arms around his neck.

"They don't call me Aunt Max for nothing."

Max Stands Up and Holds Out His Hand to Me

But I'm not exactly ready to head downstairs.
"What am I going to *say* to him?" I moan.
"How about something simple and to the point,
like 'I'm sorry'?" he suggests.

"Sorry never works," I say.
"What do you mean?" he asks.
"Well, it never worked with Mom," I say.
"She sucked at accepting apologies."

"That must have been hard on you," Max says.
And my stomach twists
with a sudden wave of guilt
for dissing my poor dead mother.

"Not really," I say, trying to downplay it.
"Besides, after enough time passed,
she usually just forgot about
whatever it was that I'd done, anyway."

But Max's eyes
go all soft with sympathy,
as though he thinks having a mother like mine
must have been a real test.

So I add,
"It wasn't *her* fault she was like that.
It was Whip's."
"I see . . ." Max says.

153

But it's pretty obvious
that he *doesn't*.
So I explain it to him:
"Mom never got over Whip dumping her."

"Well," Max says with a shrug,
"I guess some people
never get over what happens to them in life.
And some people do."

Then he grabs hold of my hand
and I let him yank me toward the stairs.
But I can't shake the feeling
that I'm about to walk the plank.

Two's Company, Three's Much Better

Max and I sit down to dinner with Whip
at the table in the gazebo.
No one says a word.

Max gives me a look.
I know what he's hoping I'll do.
And I *want* to do it for him.

But when I try to force the words out,
it feels like they've been glued
to the inside of my throat.

I cough and I splutter
and I finally manage to croak,
"I'm sorry I slammed the door in your face."

"I'm sorry, too," Whip says,
grabbing hold of my hand.
"And so am I!" Max suddenly says.

Whip and I turn to look at him.
"Well, everyone *else* was apologizing . . ."
he says.

And the three of us crack up.

If This Was a Movie

This would be the scene where
Whip's eyes would start getting all teary.
And mine would, too.

Then he'd hug me.
And maybe I'd fight it for a second,
but then I'd give in and hug him right back.

And it would be
perfectly clear
to any idiot in the audience

that in spite of everything
we were somehow going to manage
to live happily ever after.

And then
the music would swell,
and the credits would roll,

and Whip and I
would walk off together
arm in arm into the sunset,

and Max would stand there
waving after us,
fondly nodding his head . . .

But this *isn't* a movie.

So I Quit Laughing at Max's Joke

Even though it's funny.
And I yank my hand back from Whip,
in a way fully intended to show him
that I think he's seriously
invading my space.

Because there's a part of me
that's not at all satisfied
with Whip's little apology.
A part of me that wants to know
exactly what it *is* he's sorry *for*.

But there's no way
I'm going to come right out and ask him.
Because I'm scared that his
things-I'm-sorry-for list
won't be long enough to suit me.

No matter how many things are on it.

When I Stop Off at Duke's Coffee Shop

To buy a pack of gum on my way to school,
the guy behind the cash register
starts getting way too friendly.

"You're Whip Logan's daughter,
aren't you?" he asks.
"What gives you *that* idea?" I growl.

He points over to the magazine rack.
And there, right on the cover of *Us* magazine—
is *us!*

He grins at me.
"I've written a script that has a perfect part
for your father in it," he says.

"Make sure he reads it, okay?"
Then he shoves a heavy envelope into my hands,
and says, "The Bubblicious is on me, Ruby."

I wish it
was on him—
stuck in his hair!

As I head out the door,
a middle-aged woman grabs my arm
and asks me to autograph her copy of *Us*.

Sometimes I feel like screaming
even louder than those monkeys
in my recurring dream . . .

The Longer I'm in Caliphonya

The more I feel
like that guy Holden Caulfield,
from *Catcher in the Rye*.

Because
I can't help thinking
how phony everybody seems.

Just look under any rock.
I bet there are more phonies in Lalaland
than there are cockroaches in New York City.

Take the kids here at Lakewood, for instance.
Fake smiles flash on and off their faces
faster than strobe lights.

There are girls in my class
who've already had their breasts done.
I swear to God.

Holden Caulfield's just a character in a book.
But *I'm* real.
I'm made of flesh and blood and bone.

Flesh and blood and bone
that's aching
to go home.

And the worst part of all is:
there *isn't* any home
to go home to.

Last Night

I woke up in the middle of the night
and I was so jazzed
because I'd finally remembered a dream!

It was completely surreal—
all about Ray and me and hundreds of babies
living in *Ruby's Slipper* together.

I whipped open my blank book
and recorded the whole thing
in minute detail.

Then I drifted back to sleep,
deeply relieved that I'd finally
have something to show Feather.

But this morning
when I woke up and opened the book
to read what I'd written . . .

What the—?!
Every single page
was still blank!

I felt totally Twilight Zoned.
Then I realized what had happened:
I'd only *dreamt* that I'd remembered my dream.

So then I wrote down *that* dream.
And hoped I wasn't
just dreaming.

When Feather Asks Me

If I have anything to "share with the circle,"
I open my dream journal ceremoniously,
and read the dream about the dream.

Everyone in the room cracks up.
And I have to admit,
it *is* pretty funny.

All around me,
kids give me the thumbs up.
Even Colette.

Feather flutters over to me,
saying, "I *knew* you could do it!"
And she pulls me to my feet for a hug.

Without thinking, I let my head fall,
resting my cheek on her shoulder.
Just the way I used to with my mom.

Then she starts going on and on
about how my dream is such a
perfect example of what Freud meant

when he spoke about
dreams being the fulfillment
of our wishes.

And I just stand here,
with my head on Feather's shoulder,
wishing it was Mom's.

And Speaking of Wish Fulfillment . . .

Dear Ray,

If you were here right now . . . If you were here . . . Well, let's just put it this way: if you were here right now, you'd be *real glad* that you were here right now.

And speaking of you being here, I finally talked to Whip about Thanksgiving. The poor guy broke into a sweat and started asking me all about "the nature of our relationship." He looked like he wanted to say no, but I knew he wouldn't dare because I made sure to ask him right in front of Max. And Max was giving him this heavy-duty evil eye the whole time. So now it's official!

But Thanksgiving's still seven weeks away. How will I survive till then?

xxxxxxxxxxxxxxxxxxxxxxxxxxxxxxxxxxxxxxxxxxxxxxxxxxxxxxx
ooooooooooooooooooooooooooooooooooooooooooooooo
Dooby

A Star Is Born?

Feather decides we need to take a break
from our discussion of
Freudian dream interpretation techniques
versus Jungian ones,
and do some improvs.

She says it'll help us all
get to know each other on a deeper plane.
So that our collective unconscious
will be more collective,
or more unconscious, or *some*thing like that.

I squeeze my eyes closed and think,
"You can't see me. You can't see me. You—"
But she picks me to go first anyhow,
and sticks me with Wyatt Moody,
the worst Brad Pitt wannabe of them all.

Feather asks Wyatt to choose a prop.
So he digs around in his pocket for a minute,
snickering at some kind of private joke,
and then pulls out this floppy rubber thing
and plops it into my hand.

I stare at it blankly for a second,
trying to figure out what it is,
until some wires finally sizzle in my brain
and I suddenly realize
that I'm holding a condom!

A red-hot flash of lightning zaps through me,
and without even thinking
I fling it to the floor.
Which causes everyone in the room to break up.
Even Feather. That bitch.

Then, with throbbing cheeks,
I launch into an improv.
It's all about how angry I am with Wyatt
for always making *me* buy the condoms.
"Why the hell don't *you* ever buy them?!"

But I don't even let him answer.
"Why am *I* always the one who has to do it?
I am *so* sick and tired of it.
From now on, you no buy, you no sigh.
No glove? No love. No way, Jose, no how!"

And I guess all my real embarrassment and anger
makes it seem like I'm doing a pretty good acting job,
because when I finish with my tirade a few minutes later
everybody starts clapping,
even Wyatt.

And I nearly faint from shock.
And from how much fun I just had.
Is that how Whip feels when *he* acts?
Suddenly I have a million questions
I want to ask him.

Then Wyatt says, "You were awesome!"
And Colette smiles at me and says, "Yeah.
You're a real Whip off the old block."
And when she says this, it's truly bizarre.
Because half of me feels proud,

and the other half feels horrified.

Lunchtime

I'm heading toward
my usual solitary table by the window,
when Wyatt motions for me
to come and sit with him and his friends
instead.

They all start waving and calling out my name.
Which is way strange,
because before today
I had no idea that any of them
even *knew* my name.

I'm too stunned to blow them off,
so I walk over and sit down across from Wyatt.
Right away he starts telling all his homies
about how cool it was
the way I handled that improv today.

"You should try out for *Pygmalion*," he says.
Then he grins this deeply
Brad Pitty smile at me.
And I notice for the first time how
gorgeous he is underneath all that stubble.

Wyatt locks eyes with mine,
tucks his chin down just a little,
lifts his left eyebrow
slightly higher than his right one,
and presses his knee against mine.

Suddenly,
this wave of heat shivers all through me
and the sun seems to be beaming
straight out of Wyatt's eyes,
directly into mine.

Without thinking,
I grin right back at him.
But then I realize what I'm doing—
and stop myself.
How could I be so unfaithful

to Ray?

It's So Weird to Think

That I'm not even
in the same time zone as Ray.

That when it's lunchtime out here,
Ray's already heading home from school.

And when I'm eating dinner,
Ray's finishing his homework.

And when I'm still asleep,
Ray's eating breakfast.

And when I'm eating breakfast,
Ray's eating lunch.

And it's so weird to think that when
Ray was heading home from school today,

I was eating lunch.
And flirting with Wyatt.

Bad Ruby.
Bad, *bad* Ruby.

The Most Astonishing Thing Just Happened

I stopped off at Book Soup
on the way home from school
to buy Laurie Halse Anderson's new novel,

and who do you think was standing
right in front of me
in the line at the counter?

Brad Pitt!
The *real* one.
I'm positive it was him.

That was pretty astonishing in itself.
But that's not the thing
I'm referring to.

The thing I'm referring to
was that when Brad turned around
and flashed his sizzling smile at me,

I suddenly realized that even if
Brad Pitt himself asked me out,
I'd say no.

Ray's the only one I want.

Hey Lizerini,

I haven't heard from Ray in like three days. What's up with that? Is he avoiding me because he's dumped me for Amber and he can't bear to tell me? My imagination's taking me places that I definitely don't want to go . . . Please! Put me out of my misery. Let me know what's happening. E-mail me. Call me. Send me a telepathic message. Whatever. This sucks. Truly.

I hunger for Ray's font. Is that, like, a sick thing?

Obsessively yours,
Ruby

P.S. Cameron was just leaving our house when I got home from school today. I think maybe she and Whip are seeing each other on the sly. How bizarre is that?

P.P.S. I still can't believe my father's name is Whip. Have you ever heard a dumber name than that in your whole entire life?

Hmmm . . .

A dumber name than Whip? Can I get back to you on that?

Listen, Rubella, you have *got* to quit worrying about Ray hooking up with Amber. Didn't you learn anything from all those years we spent playing therapy while the other little girls were playing house? Don't you remember what I used to tell you when I was therapizing you? Worry is negative prayer. Besides, Ray isn't the *slightest bit* interested in that smut tart. He never even seems to notice her, not even when she bats her lashes at him all during math class and keeps running her tongue over her lips like she's doing a bad impression of Marilyn Monroe or something. I watch him the whole time, and trust me, he literally doesn't even look in her direction. You rock his world, Ruby. So RELAX!!!

Love,
Liz

P.S. Cameron and Whip sitting in a tree, k-i-s-s-i-n-g . . .

We're in Dream Class

In our usual circle,
when suddenly the gong starts sounding.
Bong. Bong! BONG! *BONG!*

All of the kids leap up
and rush across the room
to duck under their desks.

They grab hold of a desk leg with one hand,
and cover their necks with the other.
So *I* do, too.

But my heart's beating faster
than the wings of a hummingbird.
What's going *on*?

Is that nonstop bonging
a signal that we're about to be
attacked by a chemical weapon?

I glance up and notice Wyatt
trying to catch my eye from underneath his desk.
How can he think about *flirting* at a time like this?

Then
the gong stops ringing.
Just as suddenly as it began.

Everyone crawls out
from under the desks
and comes back to sit in the circle.

At which point, Feather commends us
for our quick response to "the crisis."
The *crisis*?

I nudge Colette and whisper,
"Do you mind if I ask you
what the heck just happened?"

"Oh, that?" she says,
blinking her lavender eyes at me.
"That was just an earthquake drill."

An *earthquake* drill?
Oh, Jesus . . . Give me a good
old-fashioned hurricane *any* day.

At least you know when *they're* coming.

I'm Heading into the Cafeteria

When for some unknown reason
Colette grabs my hand,
and leads me away from the throngs
to sit together on a bench by the pot garden.
Just the two of us.
Like I'm one of the inner circle or something.

And in two seconds flat, we're talking about sex.
She tells me that none of her friends are virgins.
"You're considered a freak around here
if you haven't lost your virginity
by the time you turn fifteen," she says.
"They don't call it El Lay for nothing."

She says she lost hers
with a mega-famous movie star's son.
She tells me the name of his father,
but makes me swear not to tell a soul.
She says they did it in his pool house during a party.
"It only took about a minute," she says.
"It was over so fast it wasn't even funny."

"Did you love him?" I ask.
She looks startled. "Yeah. I guess.
Yeah. Sure. Why else?" she says with a shrug.
Then, suddenly, she asks me how far *I've* gone.
Can she be trusted
with such highly classified information?

I take a deep breath.
Then I confess: "Only to second base."
Her eyebrows shoot up.
"But when you did that improv," she says,
"you seemed so . . . I don't know . . .
so . . . experienced."

"Well, my boyfriend Ray wanted to go further,"
I tell her. "*Much* further.
But I guess I wasn't ready."
I feel my face turn three shades of pink.
"Oh God," I moan. "I feel so backward,
so completely infantile telling you that."

But Colette just laughs.
"Don't be silly. *You're* not from El Lay.
Besides, take it from me:
You aren't missing a thing."
"You're right," I say. "I'm missing a *thingy*."
And both of us crack up.

I hope she's wrong about sex, though.

Because If and When I Decide to Go All the Way

I don't want it to be like it was for Colette.
With somebody that she didn't even care about.
Just to get *rid* of her virginity.
Like it was dandruff, for chrissake,
and sex was *Head & Shoulders*.

I know this sounds incredibly lame,
but I don't want losing my virginity
to feel like I'm *losing* something.
I want it to feel like I'm *finding* something.
I want sex to be amazing.
I want it to be life-alteringly wonderful.
And I want it to happen with someone I love.

I love Ray.
I really do.
Only I don't know if I love him *enough*.

Oh, maybe I should just quit fighting it
and do it with him when he comes out at Thanksgiving.
But what if we do it and I don't like it?
What if we do it and I love it?
Won't that make it even harder
to be living so far away from him?

What if we do it and then he just dumps me?
Like my father did to my mother.

Mom used to say that I should wait until I was married.
But a fat lot of good that did *her*.

Dear Mom,

How are things in Kingdom Come? ☺ I just checked my e-mail box. Except for the usual "Returned mail: Host unknown" message (and one very tempting offer to have my penis enlarged) it was empty. *Again*. Obviously, I didn't expect *you* to write to me, but I hoped that Lizzie would. She hasn't e-mailed me for like four days. Has she forgotten all about me? I sure haven't forgotten about *her*. Or you. I've been thinking about you a lot lately, Mom. I've been thinking about how pissed I am at you. Pissed at you for dying. Pissed at you for leaving me. Pissed at you for wrecking my whole entire life.

In fact, I'm so pissed at you right now, that I'd be wishing you were dead, if you weren't dead already.

Love u 4 Ever
(but *hate* you today),
Ruby

Weekends with Whip

Every Friday after school
Whip whisks me away
on yet another so-called "bonding trip."

Last weekend,
we sailed to Catalina.
I practically puked my guts out.

The weekend before that,
he dragged me to Legoland in San Diego.
What was he *thinking*?

The weekend before that,
we stayed in a cabin in the middle of nowhere
at this place called Zaca Lake.
There were bugs there the size of watermelons.

And the weekend before that,
Whip took me to Las Vegas
to play tic-tac-toe with a live chicken.
Funsies.

Whip never asks me where *I* want to go.
He never asks me what *I* want to do.
He says he gets a kick out of surprising me.

Has he ever
stopped to think
that maybe I don't *like* surprises?

That maybe I'm tired of listening
to the story of his life?
And tired of all his nosy questions about mine?

Max says Whip's just trying to show me
how much he wants to get to know me.
But *I* say he's a decade and a half too late.

The Only Great Weekend I've Had Since I've Been Here

Was the one just after school first started,
when Whip had to go up to Vancouver
to reshoot the ending of *Severe Tire Damage*,
his latest piece of crap.

So Max and I got to hang out alone together.
I know he was only doing his job.
That Whip was paying him overtime to baby-sit me.
But Max never made me *feel* that way.
Not even for a second.

We just stayed around the house—
swimming, shooting hoops, listening to Eminem,
ordering in pizza and Chinese food,
telling each other bad jokes,
playing Scrabble, arm wrestling . . .

I loved every boring minute of it.

"You've Got Mail!"

The little man sounds so happy for me.
And he should be:
there's finally an e-mail from Lizzie.

Finally.
After five whole days
of shameless neglect.

I practically inhale each word,
the lump that's lodged in my throat
expanding at an alarming rate.

First she apologizes
for not writing me sooner,
but she says her computer crashed

and she couldn't call me
since The Evil Stepmom wouldn't let her
because the phone bill's been astronomical.

Then she tells me all about this amazing party
she went to last night at David Schweitzer's.
About how absolutely everyone was there.

Including Ray.
And about how much fun they all had
bouncing in the moon bounce.

And about how Ray totally agreed with her that
it would have qualified as a peak experience,
if only *I* had been there, too.

Oh, Lizzie,
Lizulah, Lizorama,
I miss that raspy voice of yours.

And that funny rumbly laugh.
I've got to hear it.
Right now!

I grab the phone.
You'll still be up.
It's only ten o'clock.

I dial your number.
It rings.
You say, "Hello?"

But something's wrong.
You sound listless,
groggy.

That's when I remember:
it's one o'clock in the morning
in Massachusetts.

I hang up without saying a word,
too embarrassed to admit
it was me that woke you.

Now I'm just sitting here, gritting my teeth,
wishing I could scream it all out,
like one of those howlers from my dream.

But the last thing I want
is Whip all over me,
asking me to tell him what the matter is.

So I keep a lid on it.

West Coast Blues

It just isn't fair
that Liz and Ray are there
while *I'm* stuck in L.A.,
day after sucky day.

It just isn't fair
that Liz and Ray are there,
having so much fun
while *I'm* having

none.

Well, *Almost* None

I *did* manage to have a little fun
on my walk home from school today.
I'd just passed by Hamburger Hamlet,
when I saw this Latino guy,
not much older than me,
selling maps to the movie stars' homes.

He didn't say anything.
Just smiled the saddest smile in the world
and held out one of the maps for me to see.
I asked him how many maps he had.
And then I bought
every single one of them.

The lights that switched on in the guy's eyes
told me I'd just made his day.
Maybe even his *week*.
I can do things like that now.
Because Whip gives me
an embarrassingly huge allowance.

I've always hated rich people.
Thought they were shallow
and stuck up
and snotty and spoiled.
Now I *am* a rich person.
How weird is *that*?

Not quite as weird as the fact
that *my* house is on the map!

And hey, I didn't know that we lived
six doors away from Kevin Spacey . . .
By the way, you don't happen to know
thirty-six people with a burning desire

to know where Mel Gibson lives, do you?

Hi Roobie,

It's me, Lizzie. And guess who's sitting here right next to me? R-A-Y!

Hey, Ruby Dooby.

That was Ray. But I shoved him out of the way because he's such a pitiful typist. It took him almost 5 minutes just to type those 3 words! Ray says to tell you that that's not even slightly true. He says to tell you that I'm just a pushy bi—Hey, wait a minute!

Anyhow, we're at my house working on this mega-dumb math project together. Ms. Welford says we have to take a small object and make an exact replica of it that's 14 times bigger than actual size. We chose a Tic Tac box. We've worked on this idiotic thing every day after school for a week now and we aren't even halfway through. Ray says to tell you, "This bites, babe." And to complicate matters, The Evil Stepmom says she won't let me go to the Halloween dance next Saturday night unless we're finished by then. Ray says to tell you, "HELP!!!!!"

Loads of love from the Tic Tac Zombies

P.S. All your worries about You-know-who are unfounded. Trust me.

P.P.S. Ray's demanding to know who You-know-who is. But I'm refusing to tell him. I guess he'll just have to wonder, won't he?

Dear Lizziopolis,

I loved your e-mail. But next time e-mail me when Ray's not around, okay? So you can *really* fill me in. On *everything*. And please, don't mention You-know-who in front of him again! If he starts asking you a lot of questions, he may figure out how truly insecure I am about our relationship. Which would be deeply awful . . .

How's Project Tic Tac going? Will it be done in time for you to go to the dance? I sure hope so. *Someone's* got to keep me up to date on the continuing saga of Ray and Amber . . .

Love,
Ruby

P.S. I was walking home from school yesterday and I saw Queen Latifah on a skateboard. I swear to God!

Dear Rube,

Don't say I never did anything for you. The only reason I asked Ray to be my partner on this stupid project in the first place was to keep Amber from asking him. Which she obviously would have, if I hadn't beaten her to it.

But I had no idea how pathetic Ray is at math. I have to explain everything to him over and over again. I've been way internalizing my anger so that I don't cause permanent damage to his delicate male ego. But this project would be 14 times easier to do without him! You owe me one. Big time.

Grouchily yours,
Liz

P.S. I was walking home from school yesterday and I saw Bernie Glipman on a bench. I swear to God!

Halloween's Not Till Tomorrow

But apparently it's a Lakewood tradition
to celebrate a day ahead of time.
(A tradition no one bothered to inform *me* of.)

Absolutely *every*one's in costume.
And I don't mean
the tacky kind you buy at Target.

These things look like they're on loan
from major motion picture studios.
Which is probably because—they *are*!

Colette says that her mother
is friends with the guy who owns
Miramax.

That's why they let her borrow
that shimmery dance costume
that Renée Zellweger wore in *Chicago*.

Wyatt says that his Uncle Jack
(by which I think he means Nicholson!)
pulled a few strings over at New Line Cinema.

That's how he got hold of that Frodo costume.
He says it's the actual one
Elijah Wood wore in *The Lord of the Rings*.

And he looks way cute in it . . .
When Wyatt asks me why *I'm* not in costume,
I tell him I *am*—

that I'm dressed as:
The Only Person at Lakewood
Who *Isn't* Wearing a Costume.

He laughs at this,
and then he does that thing
with his left eyebrow again.

And asks me if I'd like to go
to the Halloween dance with him
tomorrow night!

I'm Speechless

So at first
I just shake my head no.

Then I explain
that Whip's throwing his annual Halloween Ball
and I'm really sorry but there's no way
I can get out of going to it.

And it's only after Wyatt blinds me with his smile,
only after he rests one of his beautiful hands
on each of my shoulders,
gazes into my eyes and says, "Some other time . . . ,"

only after he turns and saunters away,
that I suddenly realize I should have told him
that even if Whip *wasn't* throwing a party
I couldn't have gone to the dance with him.

Because I have a boyfriend back east.
That's what I *should* have done.
But I didn't.
What is the *matter* with me?

After School

Max and I
are lazing on two rubber rafts
in the middle of the pool,
floating in a galaxy of sun stars,
talking about life and love.

"Okay, Aunt Max," I say.
"I'm in love with Ray, right?"
"Right," he says.
"Then how come
I keep flirting with Wyatt?"

Max considers this.
"Well, maybe it's because
sometimes your body does things
that your heart disapproves of.
At least *mine* does."

"You skank!" I cry.
Max splashes me.
"Look who's talking!" he says.
"*I'm* not a skank!" I say, splashing him back.
"That's exactly my point," he says.

"Are *you* in love with anyone, Max?"
My question seems to take him aback.
But he recovers quickly and says, "Yes. I am."
"Then why haven't you introduced me to him?"
"Your dad thought you might not approve."

I'm stunned.
"You mean, he *knows* you're gay?"
"Of course," Max says. "Doesn't everybody?"
"Oh. Sure," I say,
trying to act like I *knew* that.

"What's your boyfriend's name?" I ask.
"Ripley," he says.
"That's not a very hunky name," I say.
"He doesn't *look* like a Ripley," Max says.
What does a Ripley look like . . . ?

Then I take a deep breath
and ask Max another question,
since we're on the subject of love:
"Is there something going on
between Whip and Cameron?"

Max raises an eyebrow.
"Sorry, Ruby," he says. "I'm sworn to secrecy.
If you want to know the answer
to that particular question,
you'll have to ask your father."

Yeah, right. Like I'd ever ask *him*.

Happy Halloween?

Whip and Max
and a cast of thousands
have spent the whole day
turning his palm forest
into a haunted cemetery.

They've rigged up leaping skeletons,
and all these mist machines
and spooky lights,
tested out recordings of evil cackling,
carved scary grins onto dozens of pumpkins,
and planted hundreds of gravestones.

I've watched it all from my bedroom window,
trying to push away the memory of Mom's casket
being slowly lowered into the ground,
push away the memory of the echoing thud
that the wilted bouquet of roses made
when I tossed them down to her.

I am *so* not in the mood to party . . .
But, all of a sudden,
Whip's hair guy and makeup lady
and wardrobe woman show up at my door
and start morphing me into Cinderella,
like a trio of fairy-tale mice.

Maybe I could party just a little . . .

Dear Lizterene,

Well? How was the dance? What was your costume? Who did you dance with? Was Ray there? Was Amber? What was she dressed as? Let me guess: a hooker? I bet she asked Ray to slow dance with her . . . Oh, I can't bear thinking about it. But I can't *stop* thinking about it. Lizzie, you have *got* to tell me everything! What happened at that dance?!

Whip's bash boggled the mind. Try to imagine a party without any wannabes, just bes. There were so many movie stars wandering around here that I felt like I'd fallen right into the pages of *People* magazine. Everyone you can think of was here: Julia Roberts, Nicole Kidman, Jack Black, Reese Witherspoon. Even Ashton Kutcher and Ben Affleck, and that guy Damon Wayans with a couple of his brothers. When I was introduced to Steve Martin, he pinched my cheek and told me I'd grown into a fine young woman! And Leonardo DiCaprio kissed my hand, I swear to God! I kept wishing that you were here with me. But, on the other hand, I'm glad you were at the dance—so you can report on if anything happened between Amber and Ray. DID IT? Come on, Lizzie, you have *got* to tell all.

xxx,
Ruby

P.S. Cameron was at the party, too, but she and Whip acted like they were "just good friends." I wonder what the truth is . . .

Dear Ray,

Well? I hope you guys finished the Tic Tac box in time for Lizzie to go to the dance. Did you go, too? Was it fun?

I met loads of famous people at Whip's Halloween party, including Leonardo DiCaprio, Ben Affleck, and Ashton Kutcher. They're even sexier in person than they are in the movies. But not nearly as sexy as you. I can't believe I'm going to see you in person – in just 25 days. I'm so excited!

xxx
Dooby

Even Whip's Getting Into the Spirit of It Now

This afternoon he asked me to tell him what Ray was *into*.
And when I told him Ray wants to be an architect,
these two light bulbs switched on in his eyes.

He popped me into his 1953 Skylark roadster
and took me right over to this cool store
that specializes in books on architecture.

We spent a couple of hours there,
looking through the books together,
picking out a pile of them for the guest room.

Then we bought a deluxe set of wooden blocks.
"Just in case Ray gets inspired
while he's out here," Whip said.

I have to admit
that was sort of a cool idea,
even though blocks are for kids.

Maybe Ray and I will even play with them
when he comes out here . . .
build a model of *Ruby's Slipper* together . . .

Some days
it's a little harder to dislike my father
than others.

In the Guest Room

I put a few of the books
on the coffee table
in front of the love seat.

I set a couple of them
in the magazine rack in his bathroom.
And the rest I arrange on the shelves.

I pile the blocks into
a big wicker basket by the French doors
that open out to Ray's balcony.

Then I climb into his bed,
settle myself among the satin pillows,
close my eyes,

and try to picture
what will be happening in this very room
on November 25th.

Dear Lizzie,

I'm starting to panic. I haven't heard from Ray or you since the day before the dance. That was six days ago! I hate this. What happened at that dance? Did Ray finally fall for Amber? Is that why you haven't written to me? You can't bear to break it to me? Come on, girlfriend, give it to me straight.

Anxiously yours,
Ruby

Time

Sometimes it just sort of flits by
like a bright-feathered bird
on its way south for the winter.

Other times
it's like in those movies
when people fall in love,
and in that first moment,
when their eyes lock,
the hands on all the clocks freeze.

The last ten days,
it's been more like
in one of those nightmares
where I'm running and running and running
to escape from the monster
but, somehow, I'm not moving forward . . .

Each school day lasts for eons.
Then I rush home to check my phone machine
and my e-mail box and my snail-mail box.
But every day they're empty.
And every day feels twice as long
as the one before it.

At this rate, I'll be a hundred years old
before I hear from Lizzie.
Or from Ray.

I Didn't Think I'd Actually Do It

But the auditions for *Pygmalion*
were after school today.
And even though my mind said
okay, it's time to go home now,
my body refused to head outside.

Instead, it dragged me up the stairs
right into Barnum Hall
with Wyatt and Colette
and all the other kids.

And even though my mind said
well, all right, we'll watch for a while
but we're not going to audition,
my body lunged forward
and dragged me straight up the aisle
and grabbed the pencil
and signed my name on the list
and took the number the drama coach handed me.

I didn't think I'd actually do it,
but when my number was called,
my body climbed the steps to the stage
and my mouth opened up
and read all the lines aloud.

I didn't think I'd actually do it.
But now I've done it.
And my body is entirely to blame.

When I Get Home from School

There's a message on my phone machine.
I play it back.
It's from Ray!
Relief washes over me like warm rain.

He says, "I really wish you were there, babe."
Then he says, "I need to talk to you.
About the Thanksgiving plan.
Call me back tonight, Dooby. Okay?"

Wow!
Suddenly his visit seems
so real.
And so *close*!

I'll be with him
only a week from today.
I'm grinning wider than wide,
just thinking about it.

I punch in his number, breathless.
But his line's busy.
So, I start playing back his message,
over and over again.

"I really wish
you were there, babe . . .
I really wish
you were there, babe . . ."

Suddenly, My Phone Rings

I grab it and answer, "Ray?!"
There's a short silence
on the other end of the line.
Then I hear Lizzie's uncertain voice, "Ruby . . . ?"

"Wow, Lizzie, it's *you*!" I say.
"Shouldn't I call you right back, though?
Didn't The Evil Stepmom say
you weren't allowed to call long distance?"

"No," she says. "It's okay."
That's when I notice
that her nose sounds stuffed.
"Is everything all right, Liz?"

Silence.
"Lizzie? Have you been crying?"
Still no answer.
"Lizabeth . . . ?"

"Well, yeah," she finally sniffs. "I have."
Then she says in this real wavery voice,
"Ray was supposed to be
the one to tell you, but—"

Ray?!
My heart hurls itself against my ribs.
"Oh, no . . ." I say.
"It's Amber, isn't it?"

Another silence.
Then, "No, it's not *Amber*,"
she says with a heavy sigh.
"It's . . . it's . . ."

But she can't seem to get herself
to say whatever it is out loud.
"Come on, Lizzie," I plead.
"Just tell me."

"Oh, Ruby," she finally moans.
"I didn't mean for it to happen . . ."
And suddenly,
all the blood in my body freezes.

I know what she's trying to tell me.
"It's *you*, isn't it?" I whisper.
"Yeah. Me," she says, bursting into sobs.
"I'm so sorry, Ruby. So, so sorry . . ."

I listen to her crying for a few seconds,
then I hang up the phone,
and shatter—
like a windshield in a head-on collision.

My Phone Rings Again

I just lie here on my bed
and let the phone machine answer.
This time it's Ray:

"Ruby, babe . . . ? Aw, Dooby, please pick up. I
know you're there . . . This mega-sucks. I just got
off the phone with Lizzie. I hope you don't
hate me . . . Oh, I don't know. Maybe it would be
better if you *did* hate me . . . Geez. I feel like
such a complete scumbag."

He waits for a few seconds,
as though he's hoping I'll pick up.
Then he mumbles good-bye and hangs up.

And for the first time
since I've been in L.A.,
a cloud rolls in front of the sun,

turning everything
that's warm and gold—
cold.

And Suddenly—It's Raining

Finally raining!
And the drops seem in a hurry
to fall from the sky,
rushing down in angry sheets,
shoving each other out of the way
to be sucked up first by the parched ground.

It's raining.
Finally raining!
And if this had happened yesterday,
nothing could have kept me from running
outside and doing a wild barefoot dance
in the wet grass.

It's raining.
Finally raining.
But I don't feel
one bit like dancing.
Not now.
Not ever again.

I Used to Love the Rain

The way it filled the air
with the musky smell
of earth,

the way it painted
the streets
with glistening neon light,

the way it turned
the inside of your Mustang
into a snug cocoon.

Now
I hate
the rain.

I hate it
for reminding me
of that night last summer

when the rain
licked at my lashes
while your lips covered mine.

I used to love the rain.
You used to love
me.

I've Got This Insane Urge

To call up Lizzie right now
and tell her what happened.
Because this is exactly the kind of disaster
she's so brilliant at helping me through.

She knows just what to say.
And not to say.
Just what to do.
And not to do.

Lizzie's always been there
to help me survive my disasters.
But this time,
Lizzie *is* my disaster.

Who'll help me through *this* one?

Whip Calls Me Down to Dinner

I make a feeble attempt to get up,
but my heart's so heavy
it's got me pinned to the bed.

When I don't come down,
he comes up,
and taps lightly on my door.

When I don't answer,
he opens it a crack
and sticks his head in.

I guess I must be deeply splotchy,
or maybe I look like I've been hit by a truck,
because when Whip sees me

his hand flies up to his mouth,
and he takes a step toward me,
like he's thinking about hugging me.

But when he sees the look I shoot him,
he stops in his tracks.
Just stops and stands there staring at me.

Like I'm the scene of a hideous accident.
I am *so* not in the mood
to deal with him right now.

"Leave me alone," I say. "Just go away."
But he comes over anyway,
and sits down next to me on my bed.

"I heard the phone ring.
Must have been some pretty bad news . . ."
He puts his hand on my arm, but I pull away.

"Want to tell me about it, Ruby?" he asks,
with his annoying concerned-parent look
plastered across his face.

"Do I *appear* to want to tell you about it?"
"Well, no," he says, searching my eyes.
"I guess you don't."

Then he says, "I remember when *I* was fifteen—"
But I cut him off in mid-sentence, hissing,
"It's always about *you*, isn't it?"

He sighs, and stands up, saying,
"The important thing to remember is
that you won't *always* feel this awful."

How the hell does *he* know how awful I'll feel?
Why does every word he says make me feel
more and more like strangling him?

He heads toward the door, then turns and says,
"If you change your mind about talking,
I'll be right downstairs."

"Get out!" I scream.
"Get *out*! GET OUT!"
So he does.

And the totally psychotic thing is

that as soon as he's gone
I almost feel like calling him back.

Calling him back,
crawling into his lap,
and pouring it all out.

Just like I used to do with Mom.

I've Been Lying on My Bed for Hours

Staring up
at the folds of lace
draped across the canopy overhead.

There were a few minutes there,
when I thought
I was actually going to start crying.

My eyes felt like
these two raging rivers
about to flood their banks.

But the feeling passed.
Now, I'm way splotchy,
but at least I'm numb—

as if my heart's been Novocained.

I'm Just Lying Here

Still staring up at the lace,
when suddenly it starts
quivering and shimmering,

morphing into a safety net.
And I'm swinging high above it,
inside a circus tent,

holding on to two silver chains,
somersaulting through the air,
a blur of upturned faces watching from below.

Then the blur comes into sharp focus
and I spot Lizzie and Ray grinning up at me
with their fingers woven together.

And suddenly,
my *own* fingers lose their grip on the chains.
Or maybe I just let go . . .

And I'm tumbling and tumbling
through air thick as water,
crashing toward the safety net below.

And that's when I notice a furry tail,
curlicuing in the air behind me.
And I suddenly realize that it belongs to *me!*

That I'm one of those tiny acrobat monkeys,
from my recurring dream.
And I'm howling just as loud.

But even so, I can hear the man's voice,
the man with the nice, warm, dry hand,
saying, "I'll keep you safe."

I can *hear* him,
but I can't see him.
I can only see the safety net,

see it falling into pieces
as the ground races toward me
and—

that's when I wake up.

7:00 pm

I'm still zombieing,
sitting here on my bed in the dark,
just listening to the rain,
when Max brings up my dinner on a tray.

He switches on the light,
takes one look at me,
and says,
"The first time hurts the most."

Then
he reaches out to hug me,
and I flop against him
like a rag doll.

Morning After the Rain

It's the first blue sky,
I mean truly blue sky,
that I've seen since I've been here.

It's as though someone's taken
a giant toothbrush to it
and brushed away all the plaque.

The view's been magically transformed.
There's an entire mountain range out there
that I've never even seen before!

I fling open the window and breathe in deeply,
filling my lungs
with great huge gusts of clean.

You'd think this would cheer me up.
But it doesn't.
It just makes me miss my sky back home.

Which gets me thinking
about Lizzie and Ray again.
And about what they did to me.

And when *that* happens,
my heart slows,
then stops beating altogether,

and sits in my chest like a clenched fist.

He Loves Me

He loves me not.
He *said* he did.
But he was lying.

I love *him* not.
I just *thought* I did, because he
must have put me under a spell or something.

And I bet I know exactly when he did it.
It was on the night we first met.
He was telling me this long involved story
about this time he got stuck in an elevator.

And then,
right in the middle of his sentence,
he forgot what he was saying.

He just stood there staring into my eyes,
with this dreamy smile on his face,
as if he'd suddenly been struck dumb
by my incredible beauty,

as if he couldn't concentrate
on what he was saying because I was
such a vision of distracting loveliness . . .

As if he *loved* me.
But he loves me not.
And he never *did*.

Dear Mom,

How are things six feet under? JK. They've got to be better than they are here. My life is a train wreck. Ray dumped me for Lizzie. A week ago today. You never trusted that scuzball. Why didn't I listen to you? And don't even get me started on Lizzie, that mega-skank...

Well, I hope both of them choke on their giant Tic Tacs and that while they're choking and grabbing their throats, while they're turning three shades of purple and trying to give each other the Heimlich maneuver, while their eyes are rolling up into their heads and they're gasping in vain for their last breaths of air, that they'll be thinking of me and how they betrayed me.

You don't think that's too harsh, do you, Mom?

Love u 4 ever,
Ruby

There's Been a Blizzard in Boston

And the Weather Channel's
been rubbing it in.
24/7.

They keep on showing
all these real irritating clips
of twinkling snowdrifts
and frosted forests.

They keep on showing them.
And *I* keep on watching them.
I just can't seem to get myself
to switch off the TV.

I've been sitting here glued to the screen,
on the couch by the window,
with the sun streaming in on my head
practically giving me heatstroke.

I've been sizzling here,
savoring the memory
of the soft sweet sting
of snowflakes melting on my cheeks.

And the way
the whole world
just seems to white
to a halt.

I've been simmering here,

with the sun streaming in on my head,
remembering
the delicious suspense

of sitting with Mom listening to the radio
in the early morning after a snowfall
and the miracle of hearing *my* school's name
on the no-school list!

If I have to see one more
deliriously happy kid building a snowman,
I swear I'm going to put my foot
right through the TV screen.

No Wonder I've Lost My Appetite

When *I'm* barely touching my breakfast,
Lizzie and Ray are eating lunch,
sitting alone together in the cafeteria
at that little table over by the window,
where Ray and I always used to eat.

And when *I'm* staring at my lunch,
Lizzie and Ray are walking home from school,
his hand stuck deep
into the back pocket of her jeans,
the way he used to walk with me.

And when *I'm* picking at my dinner,
Lizzie and Ray
are writhing around
in the backseat of his Mustang,
just like Ray and I used to.

Only he's not fumbling
with *her* bra strap
like he used to fumble with *mine*.
Because Lizzie doesn't even *wear* a bra.
She's flatter than a CD.

And it serves that you-know-what right.

On the Way Home from School

I see this guy holding up a sign that says:
HOMELESS MAN WILL MAKE LOVE
TO YOUR WIFE OR GIRLFRIEND
FOR FREE FOOD AND LODGING FOR THE NIGHT.

Which you've got to admit is pretty funny.

So I give him twenty dollars.
Just because he made me laugh.
Or maybe it's because it's so awesome
how he's managed to keep his sense of humor.

Even though his life obviously sucks.

I wish *I* was better at that.
I could definitely
use some improvement
in the put-on-a-happy-face department.

But I'm Not *That* Depressed

Considering that
my best friend since preschool
stole the love of my life
even though she knew
it would rip me to shreds.

Not *that* depressed,
considering that dear old Aunt Duffy's
still digging her way around the world
with that hot archaeologist of hers
and isn't even available for comment.

I'd say I'm doing *reasonably* well,
considering that Whip Logan knows
as much about how to cheer up teenage girls
as Cookie Monster knows
about mud wrestling.

I'm not *that* depressed,
considering that tonight was the night
when I was supposed to be sneaking into
the guest room to fling myself into Ray's arms
with three months' worth of pent-up passion.

Tomorrow is Thanksgiving.
But Ray's not coming to see me.
My ex–best friend
is a weapon of mass destruction.
And Mom's deader than ever.

Depressed?
Who? Me?
Yes.
Hideously.
Not to mention way pissed off.

Wouldn't *you* be?

Things I Am Thankful For

Early Thanksgiving Morning

When the smoke alarm in my bedroom goes off,
it takes less than a minute for Whip and Max
to come bursting through the door,
shouting out my name.

They find me staring into the bathtub
at the letter Lizzie sent me after Mom died
and Ray's drawing of *Ruby's Slipper*,
watching them both go up in flames.

They fling open the windows
so the alarm will stop sounding,
but no one speaks
till the fire burns itself out.

At which point,
Whip tells me to change out of my pajamas
and get my ass downstairs.
(*Did he say ass?!*)

I turn to Max to lodge a complaint,
but he just folds his arms across his chest,
raises an eyebrow at me,
and follows Whip out of the room.

A Few Minutes Later

I slink downstairs,
fully expecting Whip to deliver
an irritatingly melodramatic lecture
on why bonfires in the bathtub
are in flagrant violation of the house rules.

But he just pops me into his '35 Caddie,
and seconds later, Whip and Max and me
are whizzing down Sunset Boulevard
on our way over to the Sunlight Mission.
"To donate a certain turd's blocks," Max says.

When I see the kids there
tear into them like it's Christmas morning
and start building a city together,
something inside me yawns and stretches
and starts to come back to life.

Then we drive to The Farms market to buy
three huge turkeys with all the trimmings,
and we bring it over to Turning Point Shelter,
where no one seems at all surprised
when Whip commandeers the kitchen.

I stand here next to Max,
peeling potatoes,
and watch Whip send away
the television camera crew
that seems to appear out of nowhere.

I watch Whip stuff those turkeys
like he really knows what he's doing.
I watch him spend the entire day
playing charades with the people
who live here.

And when we finally sit down
to Thanksgiving dinner with them,
my father's eyes are shining brighter
than two of those lights that they
aim up into the sky at movie premieres.

As if being able
to make these people happy
is making *him* happier
than if he'd just won
an Academy Award.

And I can't help thinking
that if I didn't hate him so much,
I might even be feeling something
almost like *like* for him,
at this particular moment.

Monday Mourning

We're sitting here in our usual circle,
sharing the dreams we had
during Thanksgiving vacation,
when the dean makes an unexpected appearance,
wearing sunglasses
and an oddly grim expression.

She tells us that last night
some Lakewood kid I never met
lost control of his car.
This kid, Devon, wrapped his Jeep around a palm tree
at the corner of Sunset and Bedford.
And was killed—instantly.

I listen to the collective gasp.
Then to the stunned silence.
Then to the sound of Feather bursting into tears.
And pretty soon,
everyone's hanging on to everyone else, weeping.
Everyone but me, that is.

Big surprise, right?
This not being able to cry thing
is getting to be a real pain in the butt.
Wyatt and Colette and the other kids
must think my heart's made of cement
for me to just be sitting here like this,

totally dry-eyed.

School's Cancelled for the Rest of the Day

Waves of kids are spilling out of the buildings
and rolling down the sidewalk,
toward the Tree of Death.

I watch them drifting off together,
with their arms around each other,
and I feel so left out.

Left out of their grief.
Left out
of knowing Devon.

I watch them drift away from me,
thinking about how much I like that name—
Devon.

Thinking that maybe
I would have liked Devon,
if I'd had the chance to meet him.

Maybe I even would have fallen in love with him,
and he would have fallen in love back,
and we would have gotten married and had kids.

Maybe the course of my whole life
has been altered by Devon's death.
Maybe my entire destiny's been destroyed.

And I don't even know it.

On My Way Home from School

I see a broken beer bottle,
its thousand shattered pieces
glittering the sidewalk.

And completely out of nowhere
this tidal wave of sadness
comes crashing down over me.

What the heck is the matter with me?
Why am I standing here like a jerk
feeling sorry for a *bottle*?

I stare at all those shards,
glinting tragically in the sun,
and my heart just about splits in two.

Poor smashed thing.
So demolished, so devastated,
so smithereened . . .

What's up with me?
Have I gone
absolutely nuts?

Don't answer that.

Oops

Jesus H. Christ.
I don't believe this.
I just tripped Whip's burglar alarm.
And it sounds like a thousand airplanes
are roaring in for a landing on a runway inside my skull.

Which must be cracked or I wouldn't
have forgotten to deactivate the alarm
after I opened the front door.
And I wouldn't have forgotten
what Whip said to do if this ever happened.

I *do* remember him saying,
"Don't worry about it.
If that ever happens, you just—"
But the rest of his sentence seems to have
escaped me for the moment.

Which is what I wish *I* could do right now.
Escape, I mean . . .
I fumble in my backpack for my cell.
I yank it out and punch in Whip's number.
"How do I turn this thing off?" I shout.

Whip tells me the password.
I hang up fast
and enter it into the box on the wall.
Suddenly—
SILENCE.

Oh, Sweet

Here come two goons
from Safetech Security.
My knights in shining fake police uniforms.

But—*man!*
Those guns they're waving around
don't look so fake . . .

Oh my God!
These wannabe cops
think I'm a crazed fan!

"But I'm not his *stalker*,"
I try to explain.
"I'm his *daughter.*"

"Whip Logan doesn't *have* any kids," says one.
"Yeah," says the other one.
"You can't pull the sheep over *our* eyes."

"Don't you guys ever read *Us*?" I ask,
punching in Whip's number again,
while my heart does a crazed drum solo.

When he answers, I pass the phone
to Idiot Guard Number One, who goes pale,
and passes it to Idiot Guard Number Two.

Even from a few feet away,
I can hear what Whip's shouting at him.
I didn't know he even *knew* words like that.

Then the guy sort of ducks his head at me,
almost like he's bowing to royalty,
and hands the cell back to me.

Whip asks me
what I'm doing home at this hour.
So I tell him why the dean cancelled school.

Right away, he switches on that deeply annoying
concerned-parent voice of his
and says, "I'm so sorry, honey."

Sorry? I don't think so.
Not nearly as sorry as he should be.
For not nearly enough reasons why.

Suddenly,
I feel like flinging my phone
into the fishpond in the foyer.

Then he says, "Listen, Ruby.
Don't go anywhere.
I'll be home in half an hour."

Oh. Goody.

After Dumb and Dumber Slink Away

It strikes me
that I've never been alone
in this house before.
And it's giving me the serious creeps.

It feels like I've been locked inside
a department store after closing time.
It's way too quiet.
I *don't* want to be here.

I'm suddenly struck by a wild thought:
Maybe I could pack a bag before Whip gets home
and catch a bus heading back east.
Maybe I could get there before the snow melts!

That's what I'll do.
I'll catch a bus.
Or maybe I could even take a plane!
I race to my closet and yank out my suitcase.

I start stuffing my clothes into it,
but then it hits me—
I might be able to get there
while there's still plenty of snow . . .

But there'd be no Lizzie,
no Ray,
no Aunt Duffy,
no Mom.

Dear Mom,

How are things in Decomposeville? LOL. Things continue to suck here. This kid from my school got killed in a car crash. Or maybe you know that already. Maybe he's up there in heaven with you right now, playing Twister . . .

Anyhow, He-who-shall-not-be-mentioned is apparently rushing home at this very moment. I think he's under the mistaken impression that I need to be consoled. Couldn't you use a little pull and arrange for him to get a flat tire? I am *so* not in the mood to deal with him right now. Or ever again, for that matter. And I feel the same way about *you*.

After you died, Lizzie told me that as time passed, I'd start thinking less and less about you. She said that eventually I'd be able to forget about you and just get back to my life. But it seems to be working the other way around. I've been thinking about you more and more lately. I keep reliving the whole thing. Finding out you're sick. Watching you waste away. Holding your hand when you die. The funeral. Everything. It's like a nightmare that plays in my head all day long. A nightmare that I can't wake up from.

I wish you'd quit haunting me, Mom. I wish you'd quit haunting me and leave me alone. *Forever!*

Ruby

A Few Minutes Later

I'm just sitting here,
rereading all my old e-mails from Lizzie and Ray,
thinking about how I should have seen it coming,
how it should have been obvious
to anyone with even half a brain cell.

"Trust me," Lizzie was always saying.
"Trust me. *Trust* me . . ."
What a total numbskull I was.

Suddenly Whip pokes his head through my door
and asks if he can come in.
But he doesn't wait for me to answer.
He just walks over and puts his hand on my shoulder.
Which I instantly shake off.
When's he going to get that I hate that?

"Did you know the boy who was killed?"
"Nope."
"Has his death stirred up some stuff for you?"
"*Should* it have?"
"I don't know," he says.
"I just thought it might have reminded you
of your mom's death . . ."

"Well, you thought *wrong*," I snap.
"Sorry," he says.
There's that word again.

Then he says he's got to go back over
to the set for a few more hours.
And he says he's taking *me* with him.
"I'm just not comfortable leaving you alone here.
When no one's home, it gets way too quiet.
It can give a person the serious creeps."

I can't *stand* it when he does that.

On Sound Stage 34 at Paramount Pictures

Boy, am I glad to see Max beaming at me
from the middle of this mob of strangers.
They're gawking like I'm some kind of freak.

He takes me by the hand
and pulls me over to sit next to him on these
two canvas chairs with ridiculously long legs.

Max's name has been printed in black letters
on the backrest of his chair.
My chair says: WHIP LOGAN.
And, oh my God!
Right next to us is a third chair that says: EMINEM.

Suddenly, Whip's standing in front of me
introducing me to the real Slim Shady himself.
He smiles, shakes my hand, and says, "'Sup?"
"S'all good," I say,
acting way more cool than I'm actually feeling.

"You guys want to grab some lunch?" he asks.
And as the four of us head to the commissary
(which is movie-studio-speak for "cafeteria")
Max whispers to me, "*You're* the reason
that Whip decided to even *do* this picture.
He knew you'd like to meet his co-star."

I glance over at my father.
He's talking to Eminem, but he's smiling at *me*.
And I can't help smiling back.

Two O'clock in the Morning

I've been lying here on my bed,
trying to fall asleep for hours.
But I can't stop thinking about that kid Devon.

Which doesn't exactly make any sense.
Because, I mean,
I never even met the guy.

So how come every time I close my eyes
I see his car veering out of control
and heading straight toward that tree?

How come I keep hearing
the screaming screech of his tires?
Keep seeing his eyes tripling in size?

Keep seeing his foot
slamming down hard on the brake,
the stripes of burnt rubber scarring the street?

How come I can't stop hearing the dull *thwomp* of his Jeep
crunching into the trunk of that tree?
And the sudden echo of the silence after?

Why does Devon's death scene
have to keep playing in my head like this,
over and over and over again?

Why can't I switch off the DVD in my skull?

Suddenly

My telephone rings.
Who would be calling me at *this* hour?

I pick it up
and a familiar voice says, "Ruby?"

My heart does a somersault
and leaps up into my throat.

It's my mother!
How weird is *that*?

It *can't* be my mother.
But it *is*.

And she's acting like it's perfectly normal
for a dead person to be talking on the phone.

She's asking me how I've been doing,
and what the weather's been like.

We aren't really talking
about anything special.

But it doesn't matter what she's saying,
as long as I'm hearing her voice.

Then she asks me,
"How's your father doing?"

And this is *especially* strange,
because she sounds like she actually *cares*.

But before I have a chance to answer her,
she starts shouting,

"Get out of the house, Ruby!
Get out of the house!"

—and that's when I wake up.

I Am *Definitely* Awake

But it's feels more like I'm half awake,
or like I'm sleepwalking or something.

Without even thinking about it,
I slip silently into my clothes

and float right out the front door,
as if I'm in a sort of trance.

It's weird
because I'm not even sure where I'm going.

I'm only sure
that I have to get there.

So I just keep on putting
one foot in front of the other,

for ten,
or maybe twenty minutes,

and the next thing I know,
here I am—

standing in front of the Tree of Death.

My Eyes Drift Across

The chips of glass from the shattered windshield,
the bouquets of wilted flowers,
the sad rivers of melted candle wax,
the dark stains spattering the sidewalk . . .

They pause to read the note
that's been tacked to the trunk of the tree,
just above the torn-up spot
where the Jeep must have hit.
"I can still hear you laughing," it says . . .

They wander past the stuffed frog playing a guitar,
the box from a Scooby-Doo video,
the Jimi Hendrix CD,
the sweatshirt covered with leaves and dirt—
"Devon McKracken" sewn into the collar . . .

And a photo of a little blond boy,
with a smile like a birthday,
dressed up as a fireman.
Grinning so wide because he had no way of knowing
that *this* was what was going to happen to him someday . . .

My eyes roam over this shrine for Devon,
this shrine to the lost boy
I'll never have a chance to know,
slowly taking it all in,
and finally come to rest on a charred copy

of *Great Expectations*.

And Right Away I'm Thinking About Mom

I'm thinking about
how she helped me write an essay
on *Great Expectations* just last year.
Right before we found out she was sick . . .

That's when I hear a car door closing.
I look up and see someone heading toward me.
It's Whip!
He must have followed me here.

He walks up to me
with the softest look in his eyes,
and without saying a word,
he wraps his arms around me and holds me.

And, I don't know why,
but for once,
I don't feel like pushing him away.
I just rest my cheek against his chest.

Then the tears rush into my eyes,
and for the first time in centuries,
they come gushing out of me,
like Coke from a can that's been shaken.

I'm crying for the little boy in that photo.
I'm crying for myself.
And for everything that's happened
with Lizzie and Ray.

But most of all, I'm crying for Mom.
Because she's dead.
And she's never coming back.
Not ever.

Then,
I feel a sort of tremor
pass through Whip,
and I realize that *he's* crying, too.

Suddenly There's Another Tremor

Only *this* one's coming from underneath us.
The ground's shaking!

It's shaking and shifting
like the floor in a funhouse.

Just like it's a—
Whoa! It's an *earthquake!*

The sidewalk feels like a bronco
trying to buck us off its back.

We grab on to the Tree of Death to steady ourselves.
A palm frond crashes to the ground,

and Whip rushes to wrap around me from behind,
as if he's trying to be a human shield.

He covers my hands with his, and whispers
into my ear, "I'll keep you safe."

And we hang on to that quivering palm
forever,

till the quaking finally stops.
As suddenly as it began.
And that's when I notice
that Whip's hands
feel nice and warm and dry.

Just like the man in my dream.

Is It Really Over?

Whip gently pries my fingers off the tree
and leads me to his car.
My legs feel as if they're made of marmalade.
He pours me into the passenger seat,
then climbs in himself.

My heart's still bouncing off the walls of my chest
like an out-of-control jackhammer.
That was definitely *the* most terrifying five minutes
of my whole entire life.

Whip switches on the radio.
The announcer's voice has this
sort of high-pitched edge to it,
like maybe the adrenaline hasn't stopped
rushing through his veins yet.
"That was quite a little temblor," he says.

And he proceeds to tell us that the whole
thing lasted a grand total of seven seconds!
Does he actually expect me to believe that?
Then he claims that as far as earthquakes go,
this one wasn't even very big.
Only like a 4.9 on the Richter scale.

"Yeah, well, it was way bigger than that
on the Ruby scale," I say.
And then Whip and I start laughing.
Almost as hard as we were crying,
only a few minutes before.

When We Pull Up to the House

Max is standing out front,
wearing these goofy pajama bottoms
with cowboys all over them.
He's got a real wild look in his eyes.

But when he catches sight of us,
the wild look vanishes.
He runs over to us
and throws his arms around us.

Then he starts crying.
So,
naturally,
we do, too.

It Turns Out There Was Hardly Any Damage

Except for my bed.
It was demolished by the huge oak bookcase
that fell over on top of it.

When we walk into the room and see it,
Whip staggers back and then he grabs me
and hangs on like he's never going to let me go.

This is not
an altogether
unpleasant sensation.

I'm standing here wrapped in his arms,
staring at the pile of twisted boards
that used to be my bed,

and suddenly—I remember the dream I had.
I remember my mother shouting,
"Get out of the house, Ruby! Get out of the house!"

And I just about faint.

And This Isn't the *Only* Thing
That Almost Makes Me Keel

My father leads me outside to the gazebo
(in case there's any aftershocks).
And then he tells me a few things.

He tells me that unbeknownst to my mother,
when I was a baby, my aunt Duffy arranged
a series of secret rendezvous for him and me.

And it turns out that one of those rendezvous
took place when I was two years old.
In front of the monkey cage at Franklin Park Zoo!

Aunt Duffy figured it wouldn't do me any harm,
because I'd be too young to be able
to remember that I'd ever even *met* my father.

And besides, Whip had pleaded with her.
That's right. You heard me.
Whip *wanted* to see me.

It turns out that Whip's
been wanting to be with me
ever since the day I was born.

It turns out
he only stayed away
because my mother asked him to.

And she only asked him to
because she loved him and she thought it
would hurt too much to be around him.

And since he loved her, too,
and he didn't want to cause her any more pain,
he did what she wanted.

That's right.
You heard me.
My father *loved* my mother.

But

The only problem was,
he's sorry to say,
that he loved her like a sister.
Not like a wife.

See,
it turns out that Whip's sorry
for a whole lot more
than I thought he was.

He's sorry
that he and my mom had to get divorced.
Sorry that he couldn't convince her
to accept any child support or alimony.

He's sorry that he got married so young.
And sorry that he didn't
figure out that he was gay
until it was too late.

Gay . . . !
Did he say . . . gay?

Whoa . . .
I have a gay father.

I am the daughter of a gay person.
Mega-whoa . . .

How could my gaydar
have malfunctioned so hideously?!

It Turns Out

That Whip's especially sorry
that he wasn't able to figure out
how to be a part of my life,
even though Mom asked him to stay away.

And that a little bit of him even felt *happy*
when he found out she was dead,
because he knew it meant that he'd finally
be able to be a father to me.

He's way sorry about that feeling happy part.
And he's sorry for all the pain he caused Mom.
Sorry for all the pain he caused me.
Sorry that being sorry is all he has to offer.

It turns out
he's even sorry
that he's such a pitiful excuse
for a father.

"Don't be," I say between sobs.
"Don't be sorry.
For anything.
I'm the one who should be sorry . . ."

And my tears keep coming.
Hard and fast.
If it was below freezing right now,
there'd be a *blizzard* falling from my eyes.

But This Is the West Toast

So, of course, it's *not* below freezing.
In fact, even though it's December 1st,
it's a sultry ninety degrees.

When I point this out,
Whip laughs and calls it
"real shake and bake weather."

And I find myself telling him
about how much I've been *missing* weather.
Especially the snow.

"Well, why didn't you say so?" he asks.
"We'll drive up to Big Bear this weekend.
There's a foot of fresh powder up there."

He says we can go snowboarding.
And that it's only two hours away.
And that he's got a little cabin by the lake.

That's when Max walks up to us,
with this big smile on his face,
and hands me a thick scrapbook.

"I think it's time to show her this," he says,
brushing a wisp of hair off my cheek.
Then he winks at me and walks away.

This thing looks so familiar . . .
Where have I seen it before . . . ?
Now I remember!

It's the same one Whip was looking through
on that afternoon when he was
sitting out here crying in this very gazebo.

About twelve millenniums ago.

We Open the Scrapbook

And a little gasp escapes me:
The first thing I see
is an old photograph of Whip
holding a tiny baby in his arms,
grinning like a classic proud father.

And the baby he's holding is *me*!
I'd recognize that
shock of red hair anywhere.
I always thought it made me look
sort of like a peanut on fire.

"I don't know *how* your aunt Duffy
managed to sneak me into the hospital
to snap that picture," he says,
running his fingers over the image as if
he wants to reach back and touch that moment.

"You were such a cute newborn,"
Whip says, smiling at the photo.
"But so teensy.
And that tuft of red hair you had
made you look like a flaming peanut."

There he goes again—doing that *thing*.
But this time, it doesn't make my blood boil.
This time it just makes me feel
like reaching over and taking hold
of my father's nice, warm, dry hand.

We Flip to the Next Page

And there's another photo.
Whip's holding me on his hip,
standing in front of the monkey cage.

Man.
This is *heavy*.
It's like someone somehow managed
to take a snapshot of my dream.

We leaf through the rest of the book together,
and I pretty much can *not* believe what I'm seeing.

There's lots more pictures of Whip
holding me when I was a baby.
Plus copies of all my school photos.
Even my Student of the Year award.

There's a fuzzy little lock of my baby hair,
(I wonder how Aunt Duffy swung that . . .)
and Xeroxes of every single one of my report cards.

There's even a copy of that essay I wrote.
The one about my dream room
for the contest that won me first prize.
(So *that's* how he got my bedroom just right!)

As Whip and I sit here next to each other,
turning each of the pages,
it slowly starts to sink in—*all* of it.

And my heart can hardly hold it.

Just as the Last Star Fades

And the sun starts dusting the sky with rose,
Max reappears with some muffins and juice,
and sits down next to me on my other side.
Together, the three of us turn to the last page of the book.

It's yet another photo of Whip and me.
I'm sitting on his shoulders,
wearing this little pink polka dotted dress.
He must have been tickling me or something,
because I'm giggling like crazy.

"Oh, I love this one," Max sighs.
"It was taken on the day you named your dad."
"On the day I did *what*?" I ask, turning to my father.
So he explains.

He tells me that he'd been
struggling for weeks to come up with
the perfect stage name for himself.
And on the morning that this photo was taken,
he'd finally decided on *Rip Logan*.

But apparently, when *I* tried to say Rip,
it came out sounding more like "Wip."
And that's when he decided
to call himself *Whip* Logan instead.

Oh. My. God.
It was *me* who came up with that lame name!
"You mean it's all *my* fault?" I cry.

My father looks wounded.
"Don't you like the name 'Whip'?"
But I don't answer his question.
Because suddenly
I'm burning to ask another one of my own.
"If Whip's your stage name,
then what's your *real* name, Dad?"

At which point, Max clears his throat and says,
"Ruby Milliken, I'd like you to meet Ripley Loogy.
Ripley Loogy, meet Ruby Milliken."

Dad is Ripley? Dad . . . ?!
"The Ripley who you're *in love* with?!" I gasp.
Max hesitates for just a split second,
then nods his head.

My father looks like he's afraid to breathe.
I look from Dad to Max, and back again to Dad.
Suddenly my heart dances up into my throat.
"Wow . . ." I say. " . . . WOW!"
And I fling my arms around both of them.

"Yep," Max says, with a mile-wide smile
spreading across his face.
"This is Ripley. Believe it or not."
And the three of us crack up.

"Do you have *any* idea how long I've been
waiting to make that joke?" Max asks.
"Too long," I say, holding them close.
"*Way* too long."

Dad Lets Me Skip School the Next Day

To catch up on my sleep.
But the morning after that,
I'm back in dream class.
Sitting in the circle.
Right next to Wyatt.

When Feather asks us all to hold hands
and Wyatt reaches for mine,
this jolt of electricity
floods out of his fingers
and ricochets through my whole body,

like I'm this human pinball machine
and Wyatt's the ball.
Making all my bells ring,
all my lights flash.
Scoring. Big time.

After class,
Wyatt asks me if I want
to go over to Barnum Hall
to see if either of us
got a part in *Pygmalion*.

The auditions!
I'd almost forgotten about them.
It seems like they happened a lifetime ago,
to an entirely different person,
to someone I only vaguely knew . . .

We head up the stairs together,
bumping into each other every other second.
Elbows. Shoulders. Hips. Bump. Thump. Bump.
As if our bodies are these two huge magnets,
one positive, the other negative . . .

It's hard to see over the heads
of all the other kids.
But then we spot our names right at the top:
Eliza Doolittle – Ruby Milliken,
Henry Higgins – Wyatt Moody.

Suddenly Wyatt bursts out laughing,
like he just can't contain his happiness.
Then he grabs me
and lifts me right off my feet
into a bear hug.

A bear hug that practically gives me a fever.

Dear Mom,

How are things up there in heaven? I'm beginning to think maybe it *does* exist, after what happened the other night.

Before I say good-bye, I just want to say thank you, Mom. Thank you for saving my life.

Love u 4 ever,
Ruby

I've Just Hit the Send Button

And I'm about to sign off AOL,
when suddenly the little man says,
"You've got mail!"

Whoa—it *couldn't* be.
Could it?

Then it dawns on me.
It's probably just another one of those
"Returned mail: Host unknown" messages
telling me I have a permanent fatal error.

But I can't help clicking on "new mail"
just to make absolutely sure . . .

It's from Lizzie!

Maybe I won't even open it.
Maybe I'll just delete it
without even reading it . . .

Yeah, right. Who am I kidding?

Dear Ruby,

I'm writing to tell you that Ray dumped me. For Amber. Big shock, huh? I guess he finally got fed up with listening to me trying to resolve all the guilt feelings I had about hurting you. But I'm glad he left me. I got what I deserved.

Listen, Ruby, I'm not asking you to forgive me. Because what I did was unforgivable. I still don't even know how it happened. All I remember is being at that Halloween dance, and Ray was talking to me and all of a sudden he forgot what he was saying, right in the middle of his sentence. He just stood there looking at me, all googly eyed, like I was so breathtakingly beautiful that he couldn't even concentrate. And after that, it was like he'd put me under a spell or something. I was a complete goner.

But I'm back now. From wherever the heck I was. And I'm not asking you to forgive me. It's just that I need you to know how truly sorry I am.

Love,
Lizzie

It Feels So Good

To dial Lizzie's number
and hear that raspy voice of hers
saying, "Hello?"

It feels so good to tell her
that I got her e-mail.
And that all

is forgiven.

At Sunset

I'm lying on the grass,
in the middle of Dad's palm forest,
with my arms cradling my head,
staring up at the graceful trees.

The fronds are fringed with fiery red,
bobbing and dancing in the soft breeze,
swishing and swaying
like headless hula girls.

It's funny.
I can remember hating palm trees.
I can even remember hating Coolifornia.
I just can't remember

why.

Here's a sneak peek of
To Be Perfectly Honest

A completely true book,
told mostly in lies

They Tell Me There Was an Accident

Though I can't
remember it happening.
Here's what I do remember:

I remember climbing into a limo
with my little brother Will to visit our mom
on the set of her latest film.

It smelled
like someone had been
smoking pot in there.

Or maybe drinking champagne.
Or throwing up.
Or all three.

Sort of like
our living room
after one of Mom's all-night parties.

I remember
rolling down the window
for some breathable air

while Will bounced around,
like he always does
when we're in a limo,

telling me
one goofy knock-knock joke
after another.

I remember turning onto Sunset Boulevard,
and seeing a massive billboard
of a guy wearing nothing but jeans—

his fly unzipped
just low enough
to make me look twice.

Will saw it, too.
He grinned at me and lisped through the gap
where his baby teeth used to be, "Thex thells!"

Sex sells?
How does a seven-year-old even know that?
I was just about to ask him—

but I never got the chance.

Because That's When the Cop Car Appeared

It came out of nowhere
and latched onto our tail
like a rabid dog.

I glanced into the rearview mirror—
our driver's eyes looked like they were
getting ready to pop right out of their sockets.

He started swearing
in a language I've never heard before,
then flung a package out the window.

I began shouting at him,
telling him he better pull over
and let us out right now!

But the guy just
whipped out a gun,
waved it wildly in our direction,

then turned back around,
and slammed his foot down hard
on the gas.

Suddenly

We were in
one of those high-speed chases
like you see on TV—
 zooming down one-way streets the wrong way,
careening around corners,
running red lights.

Then there were *two* police cars chasing us.
Then there were three.
Then four.

Will was squeezing my hand so hard it hurt.
But he was laughing and whooping and hollering
like we were riding a roller coaster.
I was squeezing *his* hand, too,
my heart kickboxing
against my ribs.

Then I heard a rumbling above us.
I stuck my head out the window and saw
a helicopter with a cameraman hanging out of it.

I pulled my iPhone out of my purse
and a second later my brother and I were watching
our own personal drama unfold on CNN.
Will sucked in a breath.
"Colette . . . ," he said, in this real awestruck
voice, "We're on . . . *TV!*"

It Was So Surreal It Wasn't Even Funny

We looked up at the sky
and watched the guy
filming us,

then we looked down at my phone
and saw the footage
he was shooting.

For a few minutes,
we got so into
watching the chase,

that we almost forgot
we were the ones
being chased.

But then the camera pulled back
and Will and I could see
that there were six cop cars tailing us now,

like we were all
in some crazy motorcade
rushing to get to a funeral on time.

I hoped it wouldn't be *ours* . . .

Then the Camera Pulled Back Even Farther

And we saw
that in about half a mile
the road would lead us onto a bridge . . .

A bridge that would carry us over a river . . .
A river so dark and wide and churning
that it looked more like an ocean . . .

Then our driver started swearing again.
Will and I glanced up
from my phone—

and that was when we saw
that the bridge we were bearing down on
was under construction.

And that halfway across the river,
it simply

stopped.

The Very Last Thing I Remember

Is grabbing Will
and wrapping my arms around him

just as the limo
slammed through a wooden barrier.

Then that sick feeling you get
from a sudden drop,

and Will screaming,
"To infinity and beyond!"

After that,
nothing—

no memory
of hitting the river,

no memory of the icy black water
filling my lungs.

But I know
it must have.

Because . . .
well . . . because . . .

I'm dead.

So What's It Like to Be Dead?

Well, the best part is
that up here you don't have to worry
about anything.

In fact,
you can't worry about anything.
Even when you try.

I can't even worry
about what happened
to Will.

So, mostly, I just hang out
on this comfy cloud couch
in the sky

(they get pretty cute
with that cloud motif
up here),

eating perfectly buttered,
perfectly salted popcorn
from a bowl that never gets empty,

while watching Earthtube—
which is sort of like a live streaming video
of the whole world.

If, for instance, I want to see
what my BFFs, Crystal, Bette, and Madison,
are up to,

or if I want to find out
if Ruby and Wyatt are still hooking up,
all I have to do is whisper their names,

then click this golden remote,
and their lives come up like a movie
on my screen—

as though the entire planet
is just one big huge reality show,
starring whoever I *want* it to star.

It's *heaven*.

Or at Least It's How I *Imagine* Heaven to Be

Though
I have no way of knowing
what it's *really* like.

Because
I, myself,
am *not* dead.

None of that stuff
I told you about just now
actually happened.

Aw, come on.
Did you honestly think
I was dead

and, like,
beaming this story down to you
from heaven?

Then
you're even easier to fool
than I thought.

Though I'm Sorry I Misled You

Really.
I *am*.

But once I get going,
once I start reinventing reality

and spinning it off
in a whole new direction,

it's damn near impossible
for me to stop.

Though the truth is,
I mean the real honest-to-God truth

about why I can't seem to keep myself
from . . . exaggerating,

is that my actual life
sucks.

Big time.

Why Does My life Suck?

Well, maybe it's because
my father's a dogcatcher
and my mother's a meter maid.

Actually, that's not true.
My father's a clown
and my mother's a trapeze artist.

Actually, that's not true either.
I don't have a clue who my father is
and my mother's a famous movie star.

Actually, that *is* true.
Though I wouldn't blame you
if you didn't believe me.

Because, as you might have noticed,
I like to strrrrrrrrrretch the truth a bit.
I like to enhance . . . embroider . . . embellish . . .

I guess
what I'm trying to say
is this:

I
am a big fat
liar.